Petit Mal is a collection of short
aphoristic interludes
Vernon God Little.

If you are familiar with the explosive cast date
Little, *Ludmila's Broken English*, *Lights*
Pierre, you will be well acclimatised to
collection. Drawing on memoir and a life
but always ignited by the flame of fiction, *Petit M* further into
the imagination of one of the most radically origin se stylists of the
past decade.

Accompanied by dozens of illustrations and photographic 'evidence', the
stories here inhabit worlds defined by appetite, excess and transcendence.
Whether through food, drink, sex, drugs or a fantastic cocktail of all
four, the impulse in this book is towards epiphany. And the inevitable
hangover that follows. But even that (or those), in the world of DBC
Pierre, can be nourishing.

'Pierre shreds the pretentious sophistication and fake joyousness of our
Michelin-starred palaces, driving them to the ultimate conclusions of
hedonism with a ferocity worthy of de Sade.'
Alan Warner, *Guardian*

DBC PIERRE won the Man Booker Prize and Whitbread First Novel
Award for his debut, *Vernon God Little*. He lives in County Leitrim, Ireland.

Petit Mal

Notes to the outside

Petit Mal

Allegories of Youth, Wrongness and Right

DBC Pierre

Fully interactive

ff

faber and faber

First published in 2013 by Faber and Faber Ltd
Bloomsbury House, 74–77 Great Russell Street
London WC1B 3DA

Typeset by Palindrome
Printed and bound by CPI Group (UK) Ltd, Croydon, CR0 4YY

A CIP record for this book is available from the British Library

Different versions of some of the pieces contained in this volume have previously
appeared in the following publications: *Frankfurter Allgemeine*, *Drawbridge*,
Quantopia, Pestival.org, *BlackBook* magazine, the *Sunday Times* for *Médecins Sans
Frontières*, *New Statesman*, *Port* magazine, the *Guardian*, *Time Out*, *GQ Style*,
Quintessentially Magazine, the *Telegraph*, *Ox-Tales: Air* (Profile/Oxfam and Hay
Festival Press), *Gute Vorsätze, schlechtes Karma* (Suhrkamp, 2010), the *Erotic
Review* and the *Independent*

Special Edition: ISBN 978-0-571-30937-5
Hardback: ISBN 978-0-571-29838-9

2 4 6 8 10 9 7 5 3 1

Contents

Night

Night keeps me awake like the sea that makes sailors mind it. Daytime is crowded for the stuff I chase. Consumption, digestion, interaction, the distractions of sunlight, beauty and passing weather take up space.

Day is for watching. Night is for trying.

The cuts of a night are healed by morning. You can fail and recover. There are no witnesses. The ideas that drive absurdity are shut down and silent, along with their drivers. Open your feelings at night and nobody's there to question them, stain them, stifle their air. Instead the sheets of a soul can be spread to the wind. Things distil to an essence at night. All is clear and fearsome, artifice falls away. And maybe there's science, maybe dead hours spark dreams, even awake. Or others' dreams might haunt the air and be breathed.

Or it's just that we shut up.

In the night you don't care what gift to give the Schultzes. It doesn't matter if an appointment moved from three to four. You don't wonder if you made a bad choice of toaster. With a town's last bark, with the rising of a moon, I light up. Heavy eyes at eleven, trotting pulse at midnight.

And I run to drink the night.

To steal from it.
And be nothing.
And be free.

No, Sir – YOU'RE the caretaker. You've ALWAYS been the caretaker.

Immaculate

The man was going to show me something secret. Something astounding. According to him it was the unheard-of cornerstone of all Christianity. It was the Church's banker across millennia, an unplayed trump card. I was intrigued.

He took me to a kind of reliquary that smelled of must, and from a cabinet of large, square drawers, he pulled out relics in the form of yellowing, tightly rolled bundles. Then he stacked them end on end, and lo – the Virgin Mary emerged from them.

I admit I was taken aback.

I met her, and we strolled together in sunlight and shade. She was sweet, and we didn't so much chat as connect through random words that made us smile and look at each other. And the most memorable thing: she wasn't a historical figure at all, she wasn't holy, or pious, or even robed. She was just a girl. Unafraid and quick to smile. We understood each other. She walked, and her lower back had a fine, lean curve to it, and she was pretty, and quite modern. Her feet were dusty in their sandals because she had a playful gait, dragging a little, or toeing the ground when she was still. As we walked I marvelled that she was the Virgin Mary, the very mother of Christ, though from a younger day, of course. Still, what a coup for the Church. I remembered reading Roman literature from a time before Christ, and it was modern, and fun – so I knew she could be modern too. And fun.

What a coup.

No halo, no aura.

I was glad to meet her. She must know I'll remember her always. I wish I could remember where that reliquary was. But then, disappointment – it could only be a dream. I knew it. I was wearing that green coat I would never wear. Then social discomfort set in. Because in line with custom at the time, the Virgin Mary could only have been thirteen when Jesus was born. And this moment must have been before His birth. For all we know she was twelve. Things grew uncomfortable, although she seemed unconcerned. Perhaps Mary was too familiar a name to call her, I thought. Then I had to kill an impulse to simply call her Virgin. Suddenly she was so alive, so here, and I was on eggshells. I tried to recall her surname but I couldn't – maybe she didn't even have one.

Then I hit on Magdalene.

Mary Magdalene, that was it. Relief. And I was about to say 'Ms Magdalene' – but I remembered that Mary Magdalene and the Virgin Mary are different girls.

I looked at her.

It must be Mary Magdalene. Could it be?

I wanted so badly to keep our connection.

As I tried to regroup she smiled and grew coy, as if sensing that history had already intervened, as if sniffing the vast extent to which Latin art would insult her supple form and twinkling eyes, and spoil literature on her account for a thousand years.

It was all too much.

Worse for me, it'd be awkward if we met again and I didn't know her name. I wracked my brain as she pulled on the black over-clothes and boots that must protect her in the reliquary. Then she sat for a moment on a grave, letting the sun warm her back. I had to take a picture with my phone. What a coup, after all.

Our hands touched in parting, and I wanted to tell her how lovely she was. But is lovely too poor a word for the possible mother of God? First I couldn't address her, now I couldn't compliment her; the date was ending badly. It woke me as I recalled that even complimenting the Queen on a meal at her place shows disrespect, suggesting as it does that she might have served less than the best. If you said to Her Majesty, 'Not bad', 'Bit salty', it would be the same as saying 'This is shit' in a mid-range hotel. So what could it mean to say 'You're lovely' to the possible mother of God? A nightmare. The bagatelle of respect: total crapshoot due to fluctuating value. I tried to reverse-engineer the question, in my first waking moments, and define the material difference between the Queen, a mid-range hotel and the possible mother of God. Not easy, because although the words were harsher at the hotel, they'd still have you back for dinner. So there's a spectrum in operation, with floating thresholds. In the United States the line falls just below Sir and Ma'am, but we don't go for that. If we hear Sir or Madam it means we're going to be eighty quid lighter within two minutes, or be told to cease and desist. Our threshold floats just above abuse, in the neighbourhood of cursing under the breath.

The day was starting badly.

I didn't even get her number.

O sweet Mary, mother of God.

Breakfast

If Swedenborg says there's a paradise for Turks and the Dutch, I want one for poets and dogs. Because we're passionate, and know all the right places to shit.

I went to a restaurant that specialised in breakfast. It was like a frozen night club, these savannahs and ledges of tables with glassware, linen and silver sparkling through darkness. Single roses wept dew from their flutes onto carpet that flowed out under a canopy to the street. Uniformed doormen stood clear in case they were swept away by gravity.

The sugar bowl was silver. The sugar was pink.

It was tranquil when service began, staff wafting rather than bustling, to respect the natures of those who would come to such a place; a milieu apart from the bristling suits you'd expect. The breakfast set were accustomed to deference and darkness, and had time and ambition to kill. Extortionate hangovers were treated here. Captains in evening wear could phone and lie to your dates for the day; for the right consideration they would even go and take care of your business. I never found their limit.

I think the place opened at seven, though I never went so early. An important avenue ran outside, three lanes each way, and behind the hush of the day's first drink you could sometimes hear klaxons and air brakes, which in the city's concrete pastures are its peacock cries and horses frisking against their bits. Like all big cities far from the sea it's a living organism that breathes – crisp suck in the morning, warm draught after lunch. Consistent with its rhythm, icy vodka was the way to scare up a taste for breakfast. Bitterly cold vodka, then champagne. The morning's first oysters with lime. Some tobacco. And to soak up any stain of the previous day and its night, lightly fried toast with blue cheese, onion and capers, served with a shot of beef juice. Then sweet fish and eggs, cheese, breads and muscat, until by the fourth or fifth hour, when crepes and coffee were served, the table looked for the first time like a breakfast table. Just as it should, because meals are not only punctuations but statements to the future, and the dark between supper and breakfast is often best left out of them. This was the stitching together of a day's hems, sowing the night into a sac under the table; a breakfast that began by finishing supper.

Warm, ironed newspapers only came after this sowing was done. By then your senses had the balls to contemplate horror and ignorance. Chatter would grow and ripple through the lustrous gloom like early birdsong. So with your machinery kissed awake, the time came for dogs and poets to order fruit daiquiris – a healthy start to the day – and have a cigarette or cigar lit, because your demons would also be waking, and small vices entertain and distract them from harder chaos. Then carry these with a newspaper to a cavernous bathroom where music played. An attendant would step from an armoury of razors, brushes and gels, and place into a cubicle a table with linen, a coaster, and an ashtray with matches.

Here you contemplate life's bigger questions. Opulence – I say it's an absence of depression after climax. One that advertises itself, an environment that guarantees it from the first glance.

It should never press a wall to your imagining of more.

Though Alka-Seltzer and a burger can also do the trick.

Muesli

News

A summary of the *News at Ten*: shopping centres around the country continue to draw criticism for their handling of the January clearance sales, in which a woman required first aid after being caught in a crush. The stores in question have vowed to make 1993 a safer year for shoppers.

A prominent environmental group has warned that pesticides used to rid homes of common infestations may be having a far more detrimental effect on the environment than was previously thought. A spokesman for the Green Earth Conference has said that incalculable damage could be resulting from commonly used pest-control programmes, and that the eradication of certain pests from areas of land could open the way for more ecological problems down the line. He added that only by preserving the whole ecological spectrum could the future of the environment be guaranteed.

The case of Baby X, in which a three-year-old sustained injuries after falling down badly carpeted stairs, has been adjourned a second time while submissions are heard by the government's select committee on infant safety in the home.

In more court news, the libel action brought by Lord M. against a journalist who referred to him as 'the new Goebbels' has entered its third day before Lord Justice Davenport. A decision is expected by Friday, which if successful for Lord M. could lead to substantial damages being awarded.

In a study thought to be the first of its kind in the world, the entire fifth and sixth forms of Galden grammar school in Essex are to take part in an experiment focusing on gender identity and interrelationship. Hull University is to observe girls and boys from both forms wearing identical boiler suits in and out of school. Leading the study, Professor Brendan Price said results may show that many issues leading to friction between the sexes, including discrimination and even assault, can be put down to what he called 'over-genderfication' of young people under increasing pressure to adopt stereotypes in fashion, behaviour and attitude.

And finally the weather: showers gradually clearing to the east, giving way to a clear and cold night with ground frost in some rural areas. Tomorrow will begin with clear spells and some fog over low ground, with cloud increasing throughout the day. Overnight a minimum of three degrees Celsius, that's thirty-seven Fahrenheit, and an average daytime maximum of seven degrees Celsius, that's forty-four degrees Fahrenheit. The outlook for the week: remaining cool and unsettled with below average temperatures in most areas.

Time

I know a couple who spent years planning a holiday. Not that it took years to plan, but they decided to have a holiday years later. Time and space went to work, slowing life down to the speed of a community service order – but within this sentence the couple's free time was taken up by The Holiday, which flourished like an escape plot. We friends were infected as we watched. Their holiday would be a cruise. They chose a ship and a route, carefully budgeted each day, factored hangovers and souvenirs into the plan. They passed long months debating excursions at certain ports, poring over maps, pictures and guides. And as I watched I saw that this planning was really dreaming, that each hour of it was an hour on the cruise. Every so often we'd be called to celebrate a landmark: the arrival of a brochure, or a down-payment receipt; or a letter from the agent might advise a slight change, which brought urgent meetings around the table with wine. The holiday became a living alliance, an ideology, and we were like kids gathering at a ladder we were building to Mars.

Committees eventually formed to manage a series of bon voyage parties. The journey was properly blessed, luggage was double-checked, gifts, cards and farewells were delivered – until finally they embarked on the cruise.

And when they sailed away, when ruthless existence collided with years of idle dreaming, which after all must be a danger:

They had an excellent time.

Better than expected.

But when they returned home, six hundred Earth years had passed and all their friends were long dead. Ha.

Quantopia

'Donald there's a man at the door.'

'Hmm?'

'A kidnapper.'

'How do you know?'

'Says he is. Says he's come for Darren.'

'He's not going out till his homework's done.'

'That's the thing: usually he would've been out on his bike by now. I'm not sure where we're supposed to be.'

'Weird, the man coming to the door. Was Dar meant to be snatched off the street?'

'I think he thinks so. That's the thing.'

'But if he's snatched off the street then he's snatched off the street. The man can't go around complaining if he's missed him.'

'He thinks he can. That's the thing. And he's not complaining – he wants him now, says can we pack a bag, he's not got much money. He says can he bring a bus fare as well.'

'Eh? Bloody cheek, tell him this isn't the world where you make shit up as you go along. It's the one where he's been busted.'

'He says he *can* make it up, by definition, because it's reality unfolding. But he promises not to go into the version with six devastating weeks in front of the media, he says he can do the one where Darren's found shaken but unharmed on Thursday. Says on that basis we should be grateful.'

'It doesn't hold. Dar hasn't been snatched, he's in his room. What's happening is that an offender is here with a fantasy. This is the one where an offender with a fantasy comes to the door and gets totally busted.'

'Well, no, because he says a split already happened, when he didn't find him to snatch. So he's already been snatched, and we're spending the week devastated. He points out we're getting off lightly if we just let him go.'

'And why can't this be one where he's not snatched? Where he just comes out at dinner to tell us he hates us?'

'Because the man's already come for him. See? It's already branching off. The split resides at his decision.'

'Bollocks.'

'And he says could Darren pretend the bus fare's his. He's sorry but the whole thing stems from a deeply troubled childhood and it's important that he feels in charge. . .'

While mainstream physics and philosophy keep their bets on matter, time and space, quantum mechanics says past, present and future are implausible. They're paradoxical. That events can arise, happen, stop happening and never happen again, just doesn't square with how the universe seems to work.

Their argument is with time.

It doesn't exist, they say.

They say it's a construct.

Take Schrödinger's cat, the one that's either dead or alive in the box: according to the 'Many Worlds Interpretation' of quantum mechanics it's dead and alive at once. According to MWI every possible outcome to an action splits into a universe of its own and branches off to infinity. We live in every house we ever lived in. We remain with every person we ever loved, and have lived with each in every house we ever lived in, with every cat and dog we ever owned, and are still there with all of them.

As well as not there, with any of them.

According to Hugh Everett III, father of the 'Relative State Formulation' of quantum physics, we may live forever, infinitely, because at least one outcome to every event we encounter will result in our survival. Only this way, apparently, can the universe's problems be answered. A quantum computer is being designed at Oxford, and at least one more in the USA, using subatomic particles suspected of being able to communicate between universes. This is what some of the world's hottest minds are working on while we do the math of how many cats and dogs we ended up with. Those mechanics might soon prove the theory.

So, although many things in my universe went to shit, I can't even speak for yours – we can at least start dressing for the next.

'Because you can't beat the sting of that first Martini.'

'Damn right. Same again?'

'Because you can't beat the sting of that first Martini.'

'Damn right. Same again?'

'Because you can't beat the sting of that first Martini.'

'Damn right. Same again?'

Barges

Dark barges lurk unseen;
Lapping betrays their prowl;
Throw no rope to barges,
Stow all rope at night my friend,
And never rest on the swell;
For I woke after a tug,
Too far dragged to let go.

Waves in the distance soften to a lap, as waves do in the morning. It seems waves exhaust themselves in the night, and I know how they feel: glassy and barely slurping where before they walloped and crashed. The sea sends us a diagram of how it works: a goal in mind is an anchor dropped on a chain, it says, which we swing off. Our position can drag in a swell, but we stay tethered. My problem is this: I dropped anchor but kept sailing till the goal was over the horizon behind me. The anchor's far from where I fetched up. Meanwhile craft are being fouled in the chain.

Shit barge.

I decide to walk to the seafront, not so much lifted as distracted by beer. Older promenaders enjoy the respite autumn brings from the callous young; proud ladies strut on strong white shoes, gentlemen step tall like herons. The Baltic resort is a jumble of turrets, towers and columns jostling low-rise motels along a stretch of good sand. On the beach sits a suburb of *strandkorben* – wicker beach-cabinets with cushions and awnings. All are empty, waiting for humans to trap.

West along the promenade I find a wall by the beach and sit into the breeze. A majestic building sits abandoned in shadows behind me. Letters on the crumbling portico read: 'Baltic,' and a wave claps to punctuate the moment, hissing over rocks. I look up and see the pulse of a plane moving from east to west in the high distance.

For the sake of this moment I decide it must be you.

News

It's ten o'clock. The death toll arising from January clearance sales has topped a hundred with the legal death this morning of a twenty-nine-year-old Bristol woman. The single mother of two had spent the past three weeks undergoing progressive resuscitation at Funamori Medical Centre in Oxford. A further forty-nine provisional deaths have resulted from this year's sales. A spokesperson for Ashop has condemned the government's handling of the shopping season, adding that personal protective appliance laws are still too lax. Your media counsellor advises that it's safer to shop at home and pay the difference.

A row has broken out between the Earth lobby and the National Insurance Arm over the Arm's refusal to insure homes with a history of pest infestation. More than sixteen thousand members of the Earth lobby today stormed the Arm's compound in protest over what they claim are human rights abuses by the monopoly. A spokesperson for the insurer said it was in no one's interest to insure homes which were, quote, 'being eaten', end quote, without prejudice, and pointed out that over a hundred billion new pounds had been paid out on property damage and public liability claims arising from native or naturally occurring pests since the passing of

the Interventions Act in 2023. He added that it was the Earth lobby who first proposed the ban on pest control under the Act, and that, while it was good for all creatures to enjoy their right to life, we were still the only creature doing any adjusting, and that this came at a price.

A spokesperson for the protesters said the issue could expect to go nowhere while such extremists were allowed to occupy senior positions in private government. Your media counsellor says insurance and the ecosystem share many similarities, and that we should try harder to reconcile the two.

From July the first this year it will be unlawful for any child under the age of thirteen to scale, climb or otherwise mount any object over one metre off the ground. Legal correspondent Brad Neatley reports that penalties of up to ninety thousand new pounds will apply to guardians and in some cases onlookers of children found in any position from which they might fall a metre or more. The legislation follows the legal deaths by falling of sixty-seven children in the year to March the first, and the provisional deaths of six more during the same period. Your media counsellor says authorised elevations still include escalators and hoists, under guardian or licensed onlooker supervision.

The Central Rights and Privileges Tribunal will hear a sixty-eight million new pound defamation claim this morning, brought by the Association of Urbanisation Solution Technicians against a forty-three-year-old Bletchley man. Stephen Odeon is charged with publicly and maliciously referring to members of the association as, quote, 'builders and labourers', end quote, without prejudice.

In a preliminary hearing last month, Respectable Gregor Chang, presiding, said each living thing was entitled to be perceived and referred to with the highest possible regard, in the absence of judicially proven evidence directing otherwise. He said the denial of such entitlements was the product of, quote, 'low-life and scum', end quote, without prejudice. Mister Odeon has said he will plead guilty to four counts of defamation and ask that another fifteen counts of cognitive badwill be taken into account. Your media counsellor urges you to practise word-safety in your everyday dealings, or use your pad in all contact with strangers.

Thirty persons from Galden Choice College in Essex were arrested today after refusing to enforce proper clothing restrictions on the four hundred female students attending the co-educational facility. The students, some of whom are among those arrested, arrived at school wearing a variety of skirts and dresses, despite the order banning their use. A spokesperson for the college said the facility had a commitment to freedom of identity, pointing out that heterosexual rape has increased rather than decreased since the Gender Rights Act of 2019. She added that gender rights issues had gone too far, and that young persons especially had a right to a realistic framework within which to resolve personal identities. A spokesperson from the Gender Rights Bureau has issued a statement condemning repeated breaches of the Act and warning that such recklessness could set social rights back to a pre-twenty-first-century standard.

Your media counsellor could offer no opinion.

A thermal inversion warning remains current for all south-eastern trade zone boundaries including ports and tunnels. For live connection press your green button now.

Axolotl

Axolotl: we are a pair.
We failed to mature and hate the fresh air.
We both hang in the deep;
But only you grow new limbs and eyes and feet while you sleep.

Your mother and I are sick to death.

Axolotl.

After all we've done. After all we wanted for you.

So help me, we may as well drive off a cliff.

So help me, we may as well drive into a lake and drown. If we weren't already lake dwellers, and aquatic. We may as well crawl under a rock and fade away.

If we weren't already under a rock.

And fading, as a species.

I just wish the ground would open up and swallow us.

If it hadn't already swallowed us, along with our habitat.

Let's not beat around the bush.

It serves no useful purpose. Anyway, we don't have a bush.

And don't give me the long face.

Although that's what you have.

I think you know what this is about.

The neighbours came around.

The word they used was – *cannibal*.

Their little one lost three of her legs. That is if it's really a she – we won't know for a couple of years.

Three legs, Axolotl, and the tail. And don't give me the *Ambystoma* excuse. There's still enough lake left to suction your food without pulling three of the neighbours' legs off.

Plus the tail.

*

Okay, you're a carnivore. Tell me you're a carnivore, okay.

But it means insects. It means earthworms, max.

Midge larvae, daphnia, crickets, moths, mosquitos, eggs.

Let me put it so that even you can understand.

If it doesn't have an exoskeleton, don't eat it. Do the neighbour's legs and tail have an exoskeleton? No. Do they have a three-part body, three pairs of jointed legs, compound eyes, two antennae?

These are questions you must ask yourself before every meal.

In fact these are the second questions you must ask because the first one is, does it look like my fucking neighbour?

Let me tell you something: there are more than one million described types of insect in the world. There are between six and ten million undescribed types of insect because nobody has the time to describe them. There are so many insects that by the time you finished describing one per cent of them, there would be ten million more to describe.

Whereas I want you to say how many legs the neighbours' girl has. You know the answer, I don't have to tell you.

Fucking one.

Because you ate three of them, and the tail.

So help me, we may as well drive off a cliff.

If we weren't already lake dwellers.

*

You know what gets me the most?

We're the endangered ones. Not insects. You think insects are endangered? They're not.

We are.

For every last axolotl that leaves the planet, a million new types of insect are born. And all you can think to do, under these circumstances, is eat your neighbours.

You, an insectivore.

I'm not saying you made us extinct. Don't big yourself up, don't think a few legs and a tail pushed us over. They didn't, because they'll grow back. You could suck the neighbours' heart and spine and brain, they'd still grow back. The thing is this: in the few weeks

it will take for the neighbour to grow back, a million trillion insects will be born and die. And you could have eaten some of them. They wouldn't even care. They expect it.

It's the only language they understand.

You think some insect's parents would come over to complain? They wouldn't.

They're not endangered.

We are.

*

You have no idea what all this does to your mother. And do you seem to care? Go ahead, laugh in the face of extinction.

Move out, be your own man, have some fun.

While you still have legs and a tail.

After all, when Lake Xochimilco melts under uneaten insects, look how many neighbourhoods we still have to try:

Iztapalapa, Azcapotzalco, Cuicuilco, Tlalpan, Cuemanco, Taxqueña, Ajusco, Chapultepec, Tecamachalco, Coyoacan, Iztacalco, Cuauhtemoc, Cuajimalpa, Coyotepec, Netzahualcoyotl, Cuautitlan, o con los abues en Cuernavaca, Ecatepec, Huehuetoca, Papalotla, Ixtapaluca, Atizapan, Chicoloapan, Tezoyuca, Naucalpan, Tlalnepantla.

Oh, except wait: none of them are lakes.

Do you get the picture Axolotl?

This is the only lake with water in it.

With axolotls in it.

And it's three legs and a tail down on yesterday.

Do you want to know, Son, what happened to us? This whole town used to be one big lake. Aztecs ran it, and we ran Aztecs. We owned this valley, even had gods named after us. Then these Spanish arrived and drained it looking for gold. Still, this part, Xochimilco, survived. Do you know what really messed us up? Ever wondered why we're down here, under a rock, right now?

Not legs, or tails, or gold.

Fish.

Some bioscience geek thought it'd look good on his CV to run a fish experiment. Now ninety-eight per cent of the meat in this lake is carp and tilapia.

They shit, and eat insects, and munch our babies.

Your mother and I are sick to death.

You, big meat-eater, I guess it never occurred to you to munch on a fish, instead of some of the last remaining legs in the lake.

And a tail.

Sure, who cares. Right?

So we're funky neotenic salamanders who never metamorphosed, who never lost their gills and left the water. Who never left home to live in Iztapalapa, Azcapotzalco, Cuicuilco, Tlalpan, Cuemanco,

Taxqueña, Ajusco, Chapultepec, Tecamachalco, Coyoacan, Iztacalco, Cuauhtemoc, Cuajimalpa, Coyotepec or Netzahualcoyotl.

Except in a tank.

We can live in Paris – in a tank.

We can move to Ontario.

In a tank.

Go ahead, laugh.

Let the future bite you in the ass.

Let it suck your legs off.

Because only one thing is true, my boy, after a million years.

It's time to grow up.

Axolotl.

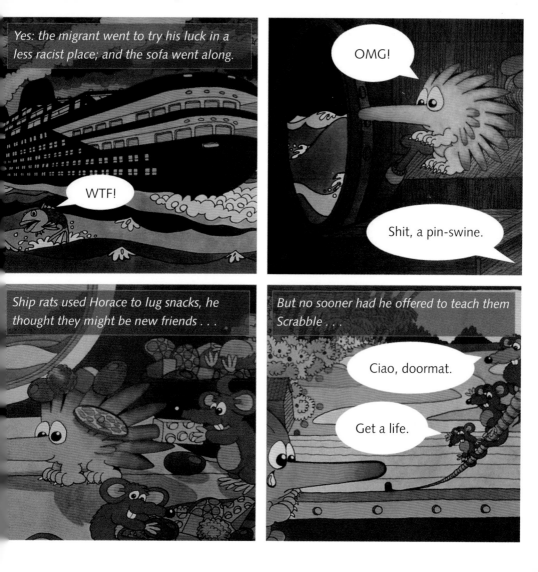

And that's where the sofa had been headed all along. As he lay down on a sack of locally sourced organic produce, he couldn't help but smile. The men were out the back saying fuck, new friends were in the kitchen – and it was all thanks to a cockatoo.

I'm leaving you

Romance

It's Monday in a house with an unexploded missile in the cellar floor. A hole shines through the two storeys it punctured. I think to myself: this is romantic.

Granted I've had brandy. It's minus twenty-five degrees, and instead of a garden or patio the house has snowy mountains within range of rocket-propelled grenades and Kalashnikov spit. Instead of a garden it has a war. I don't say romance is the first thing the owner thinks of every morning. He might prefer a rockery or barbecue. He takes me down to see the missile. We approach it as you approach quiet from a darkened cot. The shaft is there, unbreathing, sticking out of the floor. When it doesn't explode and kill us, the man kicks it.

It still doesn't kill us. This is romantic and we leave the house for the yard where these mountains rumble across a fat blue sky, and the moon flies up, bright as the sun underwater; and with this hostile border sparkling over the back fence, I have to ask myself:

How is it romantic?

Off to a gully between mountains, where two mobile homes sit across a field from each other. One is green and is a kitchen. One is yellow and has a table. Between them they form a restaurant which a single missile can't destroy; though a strike could either mess up service or kill the day's tips. The place has no name and I sit in the trailer with the table until a lady with an unconvinced face crosses the snow from the kitchen. I ponder this question of romance. I ponder the component of romance that is isolation. The type that accounts for great music, that recognises the misery and frailty of the outsider. Because weren't the Russian symphonies just cries at the remoteness of things, weren't they just, in a way, extravagant sighs?

But this place also smacks you. This romance comes from a combustion of opposites, the place is painfully beautiful for a war zone. Wild apricots and cherries will have sweetened the day a neighbour's legs were blown off. Pistachio, buckthorn and wild jasmine could have rustled under his cries. Today, at twenty-five below zero, a towel with a tropical design hangs to dry from an apartment window and reads: *Hawaii*.

Blood stains the snow below it.

Okay, it's not romance. Then it's life, the live red cable of it, the naked, sparking end.

I see the man with the rocket in his cellar and ask how he lives with the threat. He says he moved his family of six into the tool shed until the missile can be made safe; he's on a list for it.

I ask how long he's waited in the shed.

'Thirteen years,' he says. 'Some brandy?'

Shift

The phone rang six times before I answered. I was in a different dream altogether, and when I finally reached over and fumbled for the handset I could hear a small voice approaching my ear, as if through a tunnel.

It was the possible mother of God.

I admit I was startled; but also relieved. It felt warm and safe to answer the phone to her, it felt as though I could never die during the moments I spent connected, nor for many hours or days or weeks afterwards, if ever at all.

'It's Mary,' she said, which answered one question at least. It was still unclear whether she was the future mother of God or Mary Magdalene; still, both were biblical A-list, and I was pretty sure she was the mother of God, so for now I stuck with that. I had to kill an impulse to just call her Mother.

She sounded worried.

'You okay, Mary?'

No, she wasn't. The man, her caretaker from the reliquary, had been sacked. It was unthinkable, but he was gone, and in such a state of distress that he'd taken to wandering the streets in a daze. It meant that Mary was unprotected.

I sat upright. She was so real, so here. The fabric of history might rest on this moment. I would have to act.

'But where is the reliquary, actually?' I asked. 'Because I don't remember getting there the first time.'

'Cairo,' she said.

'*Cairo?*' Well – I didn't recall having been there recently, but anyway. 'I would've thought they'd keep you in the Vatican, or ...'

'The Vatican? What is it?'

'Or Jerusalem.'

'Look at the trouble there without me. Cairo was neutral ground, and dry, and full of relics. It was perfect. Now the political mess has changed everything. That's why my caretaker was removed.'

She had a cool accent: soft, lilting and fast, with a clean little burr running through it.

'I'm getting dressed right now,' I said, 'I'm on my way.'

'No, no, it's not necessary.'

'No?'

'I feel bad asking, but what I need is three hundred euros.'

Ah, now – beneath the dazzling privilege of being able to help the probable mother of God out of a bind, and despite her charm in specifying such an arcane currency, as good as asking for sovereigns or ducats – it was a bad week to have to scrape up three hundred euros in cash.

'The guardian's brother will take over until things are worked out,' she said. 'But I have to pay him.'

'Okay, but – how would you receive the money?'

'I can give you his PayPal account.'

At this point I cleared a space for disappointment – surely it could only be a dream. But when I looked down, I wasn't wearing the green coat I would never wear. Or any coat – I was in bed. The phone was silent in my hand. A notepad and pen lay beside me. And when I checked the last incoming call, I found that it was seven minutes ago, three minutes long, from number:

Unknown.

I sat still for a moment. Then: inspiration, hot as a fatal stroke. Tapping through the phone, I went to the pictures folder, scrolling past all the unknown silhouettes.

And there she was. Captured in life, on a grave, in contemplation. Half-dressed for the reliquary.

But the notepad beside me was empty.

The day was starting strangely.

O sweet Mary, mother of God.

Paradise

A stench sharpens as we move upstairs. Walls have been stripped to sooty concrete, and in places gutted by fire. Litter migrates in drafts. Some flights up, noises behind a door. We knock. It opens to a cloud of dung smoke, thick enough to burn your throat. A woman sits in a room just big enough for a single bed and dresser. Three children sit with her on the bed. They are refugees.

They fled a war two decades ago.

The war ended soon after.

There's something unexpected in the family's features, and in its manner. The boy has an elongated face and a doleful stare. Then the father arrives, and there's something strange about him too, behind his beard and in his eyes.

The couple are mentally retarded. So are all their children.

In a world hooked on the turnover of conflict, on the savage, career-making glamour of unfolding crises, this is like a taste of things to come.

The taste of a permanent aftermath.

A Belgian psychologist is here in Armenia finishing an unusual mission for *Médecins Sans Frontières*: mental health care in the aftermath of war. I ride with him, he has a jeep plastered with '*No

Kalashnikov' stickers, which is better symbology than the skulls on my snowboarding jacket. Not only is there still occasional shelling and sniper fire across the Eastern defences, but we're told the local mayor has a new gun and might be out shooting dogs from the window of his car.

We step from the building into sparkling sunlight. Snow flashes like tinsel, swirling off rooftops in gusts. This shiny place they call Hayastan, whose surnames disproportionately fill the book of human achievement, place where apricots and cherries originated, along with wheat, and still rustle wild; where leopards still roam, where Noah's Ark came to rest, where the first Christian state arose, where Winston Churchill declared the brandy finer than any cognac; and where it's impossible to pass a house without being offered coffee and chocolate.

So much pain makes no sense. But then war is only sexy when it's fresh. Television follows sex, money follows television.

The psychologist takes me to a town whose population is all refugees. No less than half are mentally disabled. The name of the town is *Little Paradise*. One woman watched a rocket-propelled grenade crash onto her dinner table and blow her mother-in-law to pieces. Sounds like the start of a joke except that it set off a living nightmare that's still playing out. The woman is still hospitalised with psychosis.

We travel across breathtaking stretches of snow to the psychiatric hospital. Between potholes in the road, and mindful there's no legally enforced side of the road to drive on, I wonder about all the mental disability. Local people blame it on certain habits in rural Azerbaijan, the neighbour involved in the war. But in fairness I haven't met an Azeri to counter the claim – and I'm not likely to, as I'm told Azerbaijan won't admit me with an Armenian stamp in my passport. What's probably true is that refugee cultures believe marriage is good for the mentally disabled, even thinking of it as a kind of remedy, a stabiliser. So disabled children are married off and left to family life, where they have more disabled children.

I brace myself for the hospital. We're met by the director, a soft-spoken man like a Russian golf pro. A table is laid with brandy and chocolate in his office. It's ten o'clock in the morning. He plays us a video of the last Christmas party, and we empty the bottle in a series of toasts. The place is sunny and freshly painted, not at all sinister when the tour begins. Then I'm approached in the corridors by patients begging for help. One dapper man folds a carefully written letter into my hand, imploring me to get him out. He seems normal, and I prepare to discover the worst. Then he mentions his high-level contacts in the FBI. They're waiting for him on the outside. The chief doctor shakes his head, we move on.

In a common room for the more profoundly disturbed, some

sitting lifeless, others writhing around, the psychologist spots one man frozen over a chessboard. He starts a game with the man and gets silently thrashed in ten minutes flat. Looking around, it becomes clear that in Europe some of these people would be on the street, controlled by medication. I ask the director about it.

'When a patient comes here,' he says, 'we're duty bound to take all the details we can from their next of kin – their addresses, their telephone numbers. But I'll tell you this: if I went to the files and phoned every patient's number today, visited every address, more than half of them wouldn't exist. The families have moved on, they've changed the number, didn't give the correct address in the first place. They can't be found. So there are patients here who could be out, but because there's nobody to sign for them, nobody to see they take their medication, they can't be released. That's the problem we face.'

Sixty per cent of the patients here will never leave.

The hospital has its own graveyard.

Next day I meet the region's chief psychiatrist. He has an office in a deserted polyclinic like a dead railway station in the snow. Winds howl through the open lobby – it's icy inside and without power. When the chief arrives, he produces plates of freshly sliced fruit, nuts, chocolate and soft drinks from a cabinet. Then brandy. It's ten thirty in the morning.

'You have to have a drink,' he shrugs. 'It's just too cold.'

A delicate tablecloth covers his desk, and the drinks are laid out. The doctor doesn't remove his fur hat or coats. As we empty the bottle he tells me there are many institutionalised patients who could be released. But he says the country is still dealing with old Soviet structures, and even older attitudes. If patients aren't committed by their families, they come to the attention of police.

'The problem, then,' says the doctor, 'is that nobody will claim them back into the home, where they can be supervised. If they're released on their own recognisance, they feel cured and forget to take their medication. They suffer an acute episode, they're brought back in, and so the cycle goes.'

I ask the doctor if things have changed much since Soviet times. He nods, and lights our cigarettes. 'Of course they have. The biggest change is that I can sit here and talk about it with you.'

Wandering the icy streets around the Belgian's base, I note there's a vibe to a place that's had explosions. Shells don't desensitise, they sensitise. You wait for more explosions. And even among refugee survivors I now find an elite: the ones who could handle that waiting enough to stay at large. When I mention the relative freedom of the first refugees we met, the disabled family, the psychologist says don't bank on it. The wife is regularly beaten, plus there's good evidence the children are abused. And when the father leaves the house to drink, soldiers come down from the border for sex.

And this a woman who fled her family home in 1990. You can taste an oncoming generation of it, a refugee culture, half disabled, all shocked – that knows nothing else, and knows nobody who knows anything else.

I ask the psychologist when he thinks he'll return to Belgium. He says he doesn't plan to return.

He hasn't been back since the project began.

'If I went back,' he says, 'the first thing I'd hear is someone complaining that their train was five minutes late.'

He squints out though the tinsel of snow, up over the Caucasus.

'I just don't know if I could handle it.'

Torgren's Travels

For those who would
know the true world
and avoid its pitfalls

Torgren

Torgren Torgrenssen was born near the allied submarine base in Borgarnes, Iceland, in 1944. He is thought to be the product of a British submariner's tryst with a local girl, which ended with Torgren's abandonment after the war. We suspect this because his name is designed to seem Icelandic, but is not Icelandic, and nobody in Iceland has ever made sense of it.

In infancy Torgren was threatened by a puffin. His hair turned snowy white, and he developed the nervous bowel which came to plague his later career as a crooner in the nightclubs of Borgarnes, where puffin increasingly graced the menu. As puffins proliferated he was eventually thrown out of the Borgarnes nightclub scene; there being only one club, it brought an abrupt end to his career. Fortunately, this 'opportunity in work clothes' prompted the travels informing this self-published work. Here, then, we present in Torgren's own words a first instalment of his guide to the famous regions of the world, so that you might profit by his guidance, and avoid the pitfalls of foreign places by staying at home instead. As Torgren would say: 'Sit down.'

In this issue: *The Southern Hemisphere*.

We hope Torgren's Travels will be your constant companion.

UNCLE GRIM

Antarctica

If reception would answer my calls I might know more about this place. What I can deduce is that it is rude and expensive, and the accommodation draughty. Local people are smaller than children, and seem to gather in large numbers, day and night. I was forced to kick one, after asking directions to an optometrist which he felt it correct not to answer. He fell over easily, squealing; so we know it is not a brave population, despite the fearsome noise.

My advice: sit down and stay at home.

Hamburg

Germany seized this land in its hunger for power – and the results are encouraging. Native Turks and Indians have been driven into the smaller shops while the conquering powers strut around in leather motor cars. Although I witnessed no actual beatings here, it is clear that a good beating could be meted out where it was deserved; and that guarantee of order is enough to contribute to an enjoyable stay. One rule of thumb: all worthwhile places to sit, including banks and state utilities, have the word 'Hamburger' on their signs. But don't be fooled: if you want to eat hamburger, you must look for the word

A thrashing could easily be meted out

'Burger' alone. This is because no ham whatsoever is involved, and never has been. So it's a truthful place as well, which is enough to contribute to a very enjoyable stay.

My advice: come and sit down.

Norway

If this place ever wanted to attract visitors, it would learn to speak a language properly. Nothing is more enervating than a badly spoken tongue, and in the case of Norway so badly spoken that it was forced to throw out its dictionary and start again. For my money the Norwegians could have kept it because the problem isn't with vocabulary but with sounding in need of a thorough beating. Not an island to visit. Sit down and stay at home.

Illinois

If ever a country showed its nature from the start, it is this one. Despite taking pains to avoid my own country's national aeronautical carrier, I found a picture of a puffin in the magazine of the American aeroplane in which I travelled. Disembarking, a youth, who looked more like an upturned clothes basket, took it upon himself to remark upon my trousers. When I took issue with him, his mother declared that he 'suffered from Oppositional Defiance Disorder', which I told her must be an American abbreviation of 'teenager'. I was forced to kick him when he thought it correct to snigger. He fell over easily, squealing; so we know it is not a brave population, despite the fearsome noise.

My advice: sit down and stay at home.

Australia

What is there to recommend this land? Apparently many things, if you can find them, because the place is as clean as Copenhagen airport, and at least twice as big as Austria, from where it takes its name. Men here sound like crows, and women like magpies, curling their words and generally warbling in dialect. The men have gone to great lengths over the years to spread an image of rugged independence, but the place is run by women, as the same lengths would suggest. A man here becomes nervous to accept beer after a certain time, and this is because his wife has put in his mind a time by which he must leave in his truck. Also the laws in this land are made by women, who could easily mete out a beating where one was deserved. To make contact with one's wife under her clothes can be charged as rape, just as firmly as if she had been tackled in an alley. Australia having been an open prison in Austro-Hungarian times, it continues to define itself by suspicion and law.

My wife was most comfortable here, which in turn was enough to contribute to an enjoyable stay. Fish are good in Austria, and hospitality is very great, as her people have been condemned away for a long time, and welcome any new face. After a warm greeting in this way, they quickly return to their business of monitoring and charging each other with offences. Biting parrots infest the north.

Come and sit down, with women.

Turkey

I tried to buy a rug here and the man made contact with my wife beneath her clothes, and in a sweaty way. Constantinople is the capital, and is noisy with the cries of people trapped in towers. These are a people of hanging eyes and much swarthe about the face. They don't shave and drink a shocking coffee.

Sit down and stay at home.

Italy

Wherever in God's name the Romans found models for their statues, it wasn't Rome, as these are a people of hanging eyes and much swarthe about the face. Models could only have come down from Milan for the job, or the whole empire has been mistaken for Greece. Our taxi was driven by a man shorter than my wife's mother, and rounder by far, who found all of life so amusing that I was forced to kick him. He fell over easily, squealing; so we know it is not a brave population, despite the fearsome noise.

My advice: sit down and revise your memory of Caesar.

Scotland

Fearsome beatings can be meted out here, and are even expected by this hardy, short-lived people, who speak almost perfect Icelandic after taking a drink. I was forced to kick one and he flew back at me, causing a change of dress before dinner. I was affectionately called Knut, in the old pronunciation, by the brave population, who managed to guess this pet name without contacting each other at all. Even my wife was using it by the end of our visit, 'Old Knut' rang across the streets of the island, and it was enough to contribute to an enjoyable stay.

My advice: come and sit down.

This concludes the famous regions of the southern hemisphere.

In Iceland Man stands alone against all the might of nature, which equips him well to travel and bring order to the mayhem and dishonesty of foreign parts. Torgren is currently at work on his guide to the northern hemisphere, including only Greenland. Until then: 'Sit down.'

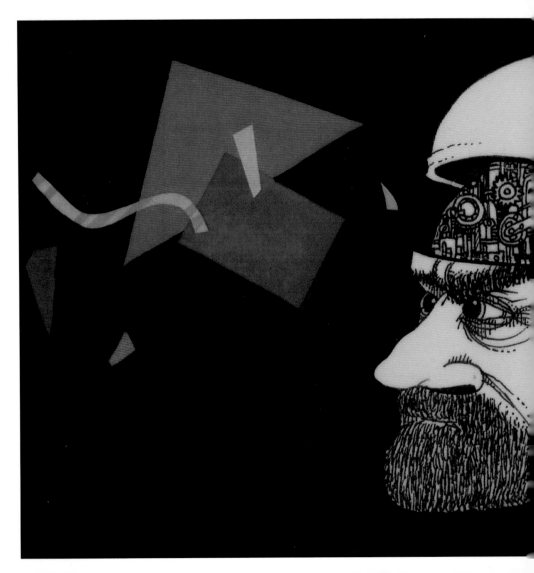

Conversion

My friends were heavy sleepers. Or rather, we did things that led to heavy sleep. It was a drag to wake any of us, but we took turns trying. Until finally one of us hit on a way that used no volume or violence. We found that dropping a bent idea into the sleeping brain would cause it to wake. We just had to say, urgently but reasonably, something like, 'The exhaust pipe's frozen.'

The mind has to break surface to deal with this.

I was reminded of it one morning a couple of years ago. I came out of bed to find an email from someone called Vinko Gorski. I'm not bright in the morning, days for me are tiny lifetimes, starting dumb and fragile. Then this email began: 'I'm a bit seduced to understand everything, but despaired also so I would ask for your help, rising to become really annoying.'

After coffee I read some more: 'Boy, this story has really bomb under the back, but I don't respect to put only tit issues for the boy, but make also serious topic. I hope is not just making you dull so many boring questions.'

Some time before that morning my first novel, *Vernon God Little*, had been published. Gorski was a translator. Vernon was translated into some forty languages but it happened gradually, I joined a growing network of linguists tackling its made-up slang. The exercise showed that we live in worlds built from the ideas inside words; self-expanding concepts with their own climate and colour. Some translators questioned me a lot, others barely so, some I never heard from. The French found a brilliant American Francophile to do it, the Germans an East Berlin hiphopper, the Dutch a man who took clues from Italian.

Some found it easier than others.

Vernon God Little is about a teenager having a hard time in Texas. His father is dead. The book's subplot holds clues to the father's death and the whereabouts of the body. Perhaps more than some books, *Vernon* is one you either get or don't get.

Gorski wrote to me from a small ex-Soviet state, explaining that he had six months to translate the book. It was soon after *Vernon* won the Man Booker Prize, and I was lost in a vortex of activity, from Rome to Reykjavik to Rio. But I don't think a day passed without mail from Gorski.

'Boy, Pierre, on this subject of cursing, when you leave the childish western way and try Slavic curse you really know what it's all for, boy, like some drunkards in my neighbourhood.' Or, 'I wonder what is exactly meaning of "jacket"? Obvious it could mean three differently – at least here we have three different: the short coat, or the sportish, unofficial, mainly for teenage and low-middle classes; or like in *Top Guns*, for even woman with skirt. I hear even writer like to wear these coat, but without skirt, ha ha ha.'

I must have rewritten the book twice over in paraphrased emails to Gorski, trying to explain that sometimes a knock at the door is just a knock at the door, and that whatever wood the door is made from didn't move the narrative along. But it wasn't good enough for Vinko Gorski. He had a trump card, which was his unique native tongue.

'Ah, no, but you see, here we can say "Knock", or we can say "*Knock*", and also say more like "Batter", and even "Trounce", which is like seriously knock.'

'Vinko, just say he rang the doorbell. The important thing here is that the scene won't start until someone opens the door.'

'Good, yes, fine, always the writer has the good idea, ha ha ha. But is it doorbell – or door-*music*? Because here we can say . . .'

After half a lifetime, even after Gorski had delivered his work to the publisher, he would write to say: 'Me again, hovering with silly question. Still no news from publisher but meanwhile my wife start with the draft and make some good question.'

I stuck with Gorski, as I did with every translator. I came to see that a creative work isn't even just a set of ideas, but also a type of shine – its radiated light was what a good translator would try to capture, filtering it up or down the spectrum.

But then some translators have a spectrum all their own.

In the last days of correspondence with Gorski, after no less than a year's work, he said his translation had been accepted by the publisher, and was on its way to press.

'Just only for my small interest,' he wrote, 'one thing I wonder for myself – why Vernon's father never comes to his house?'

'Vinko,' I replied. 'The father is dead.'

And after two or three days, Gorski's shortest mail yet.

'Oh shit.'

This DNA test will tell us whether Jason is lying

Otter

There's a giant otter in County Leitrim. The Master Otter, or *Dobhar-Chú*, has blood on its paws according to centuries of local history. A killer master otter. It's been called the Irish crocodile.

Try sitting on the bank of a snarling river, with gales knotting your hair, and see if you don't want to ask about the otter. It's a fact that certain otters grow to six feet. A fact that at least two headstones in Leitrim name victims of the master otter – one even shows *Dobhar-Chú* being impaled by a spear.

I try asking a farmer from around the mountain. I ask him about the man-eating otter and wait for him to collapse laughing. But he doesn't, he frowns, this stormy evening.

'Otter?' he says. 'Well, I was stopped on the bridge Tuesday – you know the bridge there, by the bend?'

'Uh-huh.'

'Except I couldn't stop long, my auld bitch was after bleeding something fierce.'

'You were going to the vet?'

'Not at all, the vet couldn't do nothing. Dog bled all night till her blanket was soaked, then bled a night still. Thought it was her end.'

'So what happened?'

'Well,' he muses. 'I took her for a cure.'

'Oh?'

'Aye, just. A woman in the village has a powerful cure.' He waits to see if I collapse laughing. 'It's a prayer, written on a scrap of paper. You tie it to the dog's tail. By morning the bleeding stopped. Auld dog woke up fine, as if nothing.'

'That's some old woman.'

'Not at all, young filly. But it will have been passed on.'

'The cure? By her mother?'

'Ach, t'will have been a man. A woman can't pass a cure to another woman, nor a man to another man. Could've been her uncle passed it on. You never can know which way t'will travel.'

'Uh-huh. So this otter . . .'

'Aye, you know the bridge there – the one with all the frogs? You'll see awful amounts of frogs there just now.'

'I have seen a lot of frogs lately.'

'Aye, just. And if you watch them, you'll see the one-year-olds killing the two-year-olds. See how the young kill the auld frogs?'

I admit I haven't. His eyes light up. 'The one-year-olds climb onto the backs of the two-year-olds, they hang on till the auld frog's stopped dead from exhaustion. If you go up the mountain, up by the antenna, you'll see them.'

'The antenna's a lightning rod in this weather.'

'Aye, just. Like a horse.'

'Eh?'

'Aye, a horse will attract lightning. A horse will attract it, but a cow'll not. Although I can hear the bells of Drumshanbo church at my place. If you can hear the bells you're alright, there's never a lightning strike within earshot of the bells . . .'

Warning

The rumour spoke of a sandwich. It said it was egg and cress. But I didn't immediately covet the sandwich, as word ran through the crowd. Instead I felt a fleeting violence towards the type of person who spends too long in front of the sandwich cabinets in shops. They stand and examine one after another sandwich in case the tomato has soaked the bread or the chicken has gone dry. Stand there, agonising, blocking the sandwich you want to take, this type of person. In a reasonable world the sandwich blocker would be a minor irritation. But in the tunnel I felt a harder violence.

Probably because I was one.

And that, I thought, is today: frustration turned to irritation turned to violence, towards others whose irritation has turned the same way. This is the type of person I'm down here with. Others like me, forced to hear of a sandwich.

Every hour wounds and the last one kills – plus someone might have a sandwich. Strange to note how divided my instincts became – between the impulse to trample bodies, and a helicopter view of how the rumours spread. In the first two hours we survived on rumours alone. They were self-seeding and self-inflating. They started ambitiously, within an hour of the incident, with the whisper that huge ventilation fans had been installed at each end of the tunnel. Some people even said they felt a breeze, and we soon thought we could see a breeze lift their hair.

But there were no fans.

If there was an egg and cress sandwich down here you would smell it, and if eaten, you would smell who ate it. Though it might still be packaged and sealed. You could feel these thoughts wash through the tunnel behind the rumour, everyone imagining a plastic triangle stuffed with sandwich. Perhaps business-class passengers imagined a recycled cardboard triangle with an ethos printed on it, from a company called Vuzu or Goozoo or Zazz.

But it was a sandwich. The tunnel quivered like an anemone reef around the rumour. Until we heard of someone with mobile phone signal, which was a rumour that flashed this way and that like a shoal of fish. For myself, I cling to this morning's rumour: that Terminal Three has been secured, and the army is freeing us one by one, after security screening. I also say it because I could swear I'm a yard farther along this walkway.

I still curse between rumours. Not the authorities, but the geniuses who think that a threat of collapse to a culture in collapse is any threat. Today proves it: you don't need bombs to make us hysterical. Just rumours.

Obviously there are lesser curses too. The rail system that

couldn't get me here earlier, which would have seen me in the last passenger intake for the terminal.

I look down the tunnel. Not only sandwich blockers, there are bullish Americans, angry French, and the hundred Italian students who started the crush in the first place – not because a train wasn't there to board, but because they couldn't understand the one working ticket machine.

And we all know it's an offence to board without a valid ticket.

I listen over and over to the recording warning us that the end of the moving walkway is near. It accompanies the sign on the wall warning that threats, violence and abusive language will not be tolerated. The walkway's not even moving but still this crisp, disembodied voice drones on and on, this British voice with the airs of a 1950s that never existed, voice from a Britain that never was.

But she's always been here. Threatening us from loudspeakers. Maybe that's why neither bombs nor rumours are any real threat to our way of life.

Our way of life is the end of the moving walkway now approaching. Just look around.

Like we needed reminding.

Dick

You made it unfashionable to speak in clear terms, but I'm going to do it here. I'm also going to humanise something you do, which will really fuck up your business model. You see, Richard – I'll call you Dick – I've worked out who you are. You probably thought I'd forget, we met so long ago; or more likely you thought there was nothing to forget, as in your world only that which convinces is fact, and you were convincing. But you're of my ilk. We were children together, and children never forget people like you.

What I remember, Dick, is that you were the kid who punched me then swore on his mother's grave that he hadn't. I saw you do it. Nobody else was there. And when I asked why, you launched an argument that left me questioning my own judgement. By the end you'd even painted me the enemy; how could I believe you'd do such a thing? What kind of animal was I?

Your injured pride was genuine. Scary, Dick.

Now you've grown up and come to power. I can tell because the streets reek of the same gaslight; what you do is gaslighting, Dick, blurring our sense of fact so you can replace it with yours. You grew up doing it to impress yourself with how convincing you sounded. You didn't have to actually do anything in life, just saying that you did it was convincing enough.

So you invented an industry. Not only a job for yourself, you also convinced anyone else without a skill that manipulating reality was the new black. This is why I'm writing to you. It's time for us to distinguish between what we do, and what we merely appear to do. Doing is doing and appearing to do is only appearing to fucking do it, Dick. If you punch me, you punch me. If you punch me and convince me that you didn't, you still punched me. It's not as if you're even trying to change the world; you're just trying to convince me you didn't punch me. Because let's be real: did you go this way to improve the human lot? No, you did it for an Audi. Now you have the Audi and you're not stopping until you reach a Gulfstream jet, which means you're not stopping, because you're just not that convincing.

But it's over, Dick. You've empowered a generation to do this, and there aren't that many Gulfstream jets. All there are now are cardboard offices where you brainstorm ways to tell us black is white. Black is black, Dick. You punched us all and we remember you. Everyone who reads this will remember you. It's time to accept that the world you designed is a slum fuelled by weakness and pathology. It's time to accept that everything you promise leaves us vaguely empty at best.

Because it is untrue.

That's the only fact, Dick. Plus one exquisite irony: you pictured us as organisms with the indifference of callous nature, to be harvested for your gain – and it made us callously indifferent to you. Did we start out that way? No. The truth is that only you were indifferent like callous nature. Only *you* were, Dick.

But you talked us around.

No terms and conditions applied.

And now, when you next feel a punch –

It wasn't us, we swear.

Lie

Robert brought a skeleton to school. It came in supermarket bags, burial tatters still hung off the bones. Our biology teacher once wished for an anatomical model; so Robert dug one up.

Harsh, even by sixth-form standards. And it exposed Robert. We knew he was weird, like we were weird, he was usually our cover – but if he spilled too far into the real world we couldn't help him. Giving the bags to the teacher would be spilling way out. He would never understand this – that's the heart of all weirdness: in his mind it had logic, it precisely fitted the teacher's wish, and anyway was a kind of recycling. But when the rest of us looked in the bags we knew he had his work cut out. We knew it was the kind of trouble that runs through a school in whispers. He needed a grand lie. He would have to give it a soft history, an aura of chance, of romance.

Robert was weird but he was honest. Not that he wouldn't blurt shit out, but he laid no groundwork for his higher schemes. We can only wonder how he missed the clues. Maybe his parents hadn't rescinded the tooth fairy. Maybe teachers had trampled his every half-truth, because let's be honest about honesty, it's parents and teachers who configure acceptable truth; and they don't teach not to lie – simply when, and how. Like birds, from little brown ones in the service of apathy to the flightless hulks of politics and the Public Good, life is cooled by the wing beats of lies.

Robert just didn't care. Maybe that's why we loved him.

The biology teacher was a gentle, cultured woman who spoke Russian and wrote books and knew her Brahms. Robert came leering up to her and opened the bags in her face. She recoiled and asked where they were from – and he said the cemetery.

The truth. An honourable thing.

We didn't see Robert for a long time after that.

Now observe a master: the one who skipped all of exam week and returned with a price on his head. His excuse made you blink a few times, I admit. But it worked. He said his family had been kidnapped by leftist insurgents in the south. Within a minute he was back in the common room, laughing, and the subject was never raised again. Let's examine how.

First, he knew that the stresses of correcting him were not in a teacher's real interests, and he wasn't disliked enough to invite much effort in prosecution. He also knew he had to reward his audience in some way. To do this he followed the lead of governments in heeding Adolf Hitler – that the great masses of the people will more easily fall victim to a great lie than to a small one. His gift was not only a well-structured lie – it was a whopper. A lie so cumbersome, so improbable, that to question it would be to question his whole bloodline. His gift to them was an *obvious* lie. Something that would cover the teacher's back, something with a ripcord, also something implausible enough to form a token of penance, an unforgettable weight on the liar's back.

It wasn't a cheap lie. But its real genius was this: he didn't tell it himself. He let third parties tell it. Before his return to school he let the news slip to the most gullible, chattering minions, and they did the job before he appeared. The perfection in this is that even the gullible recognise implausibility; it's just that their drive to earn kudos through gossip is stronger, so that given the licence to spread a rumour, they polish it, add their personal guarantees, and make it airtight in order not to look stupid. And so a rabid murmur spread through school one day, gaining texture and becoming real. By the time the lie's author came through the gate, faces just fell in sympathy; he just had to crease his brow.

A bravura performance.

Years after Robert brought the bones to school, I returned and saw the skull being used for still-life drawing in the art department. When I asked the assistant where it came from, he said an auction of educational materials.

And that's a lie.

Angels

He has the stare of a kid watching a murder. It seems permanent. We meet at midnight next to the angel of independence: an angel of gold in the heart of the city.

'I wouldn't call us vampires,' he warms his hands on a take-away coffee. 'Maybe angels of death.'

Five cohorts hang around leaning on cars. One is dressed as a gangster, with topcoat, hat and a moll in Deco furs on his sleeve. Six nights a week they gather here in a hunting pack, monitoring radio-scanner traffic, staring into the night, waiting to scramble. They're journalists for Mexico's death press.

'Stabbing, *San Felipe*,' one deciphers a numbered code from the emergency chatter. 'Not breathing!'

We fly across the city in convoy, running red lights, stop signs, one-way streets, trailing a comet-tail of hazard blinkers. Death – now more urgent than life. You look around this teeming organism and wonder about its ability to contemplate horror. Different layers of history here had different tastes for death; now they're all in a dance together, still feeding on blood. The Conquistadors arrived to find Aztecs up to their necks in human sacrifice. They were so disgusted they replaced it with the Church, which until recently would dig up and exhibit your loved ones' naked corpses to the public if you didn't pay the rent on their graves. Not far away in the south of the city an old convent still displays its mummies, preserved by mysterious air and soil.

You still have to pay to see them.

Aztecs and Christians do an extended mix of this at Halloween. Add in trick-or-treating children with horror masks and you have all your darkest fears performed and celebrated by a cast of millions. Day of the Dead is an all-night rave with crosses, skulls, tequila and incense, and the church at Mixquic is its hard core – a yard awash with human bones, a baptismal font carved into an altar once used to sacrifice children. Aztecs were materialistic, they paid for a god's favours, mostly in blood – but this altar's chill would also shock valuable tears from an infant, encouraging rain.

Before they got down to the blood.

History may be macabre but today's necromancy seems cosy, kitsch, retro-baroque; even healthy, with skeleton icons as charming as collectable frogs, pushing prams, playing trumpets, misbehaving. Even the death press has its place in society, an additional watchdog over the shadows.

This night a police car beats us to the stabbing. Another man in gangster-wear turns up separately, chewing on a cigar; but this man has two barrels of a pump-action shotgun poking from his topcoat.

His demeanour says the death belongs to him.

The detective's arrival is some kind of defeat for my angels. He's an anticlimax that dulls the returning convoy. No blinkers, no red lights, no conversation. I don't even want to wonder why we needed the body to ourselves. A shrine to *Santa Muerte* – Saint Death, the skeleton in virgin's robes – flashes by. Originally a patron saint for delinquents offering prayers before a crime, she now succours souls across the culture. She's a return to Aztec materialism, a conga line through the Church and out the back door to the volatile humours that always governed here.

You can feel them in the air. They sizzle with a power that reason has no answer for, that science can't dare to touch.

The radio suddenly crackles. 'Crash on *Viaducto*!'

Phone screens light the car like a pinball machine as a web of informants phones in, scampering to confirm the victim's condition.

But faces soon fall.

'Shit. A broken leg.'

Pharmageddon

You know it's a hard party when your dog has a breakdown. Years passed before I understood that summer. Across a span of months certain friends and strangers and I reversed civilisation, we spat the childhood out of my childhood home.

The dog never understood. *We* never understood, if it was self-destruction or self-creation. It fed automatically on the vacuum left by absent parents. But if it was destruction what did it destroy? If it was creation what did it create? These are the questions.

The summer cost a friend's life, and a dog, and asked these questions. Summer of the End Party, a centrifuge that spewed us onto a decade and into a life. The setting was a mansion behind walls topped with broken glass. The dog was a timberwolf–husky cross, ghostlike, with ice-blue eyes, who saw things that weren't there. There were staff, including Maria, who learned to frisk laundry for drugs before washing it. It was the summer when everyone seemed to be kicked out of their houses. They smelled an empty mansion and came one by one, and knew others who, if they weren't already kicked out, would benefit from lessening their footprint at home. From this gene pool a taste grew for the abyss. We were newborn and our god was oblivion.

There was Danny with the red eyes who made a home with a bottle of tequila on the floor beside a balcony where he kept saying, 'The moon's a balloon.' He said it every day. He was probably expelled from home for saying it. We always waited for him to say it, and the day would light up when he did. Nobody knew what else was inside him. Nobody even knew who else knew him, or if anyone knew him.

He was just there.

There was Cesare, banished for throwing a typewriter at the teacher on his hospitality course, then having a thug bring a gun to talk the teacher out of reporting him to his parents. He had a copy of the *Physicians' Desk Reference*, and we became doctors. Tony then proved that pharmacies would deliver drugs on a bike if you called saying you were a doctor. He proved they would deliver Marlboro as well. Who knows if the pharmacist heard *Fly Like an Eagle* playing in the background when we called.

The thing about decadence: we hunted higher oblivion every day for the same reason people climb mountains, except the ethos was reversed. We climbed because it wasn't there.

I look back and see we had one thing in common: a loss of trust. A loss of hope and trust in the scheme of things. In the parents, in the suits. Like dogs betrayed we were trashing expectations of us. We made a craft of their trashing.

So it was destruction then.

We did it because expectations hadn't worked for us.

We tried them and were unsuccessful.

So we found this thing at which we were successful. Nobody ever phoned to say we were doing it wrong. It was a job. Oblivion is hard work, it takes commitment. It takes qualities likely to bring success in any other field, including in a suit. But we spent that energy running the other way.

Ours wasn't a reaction to hard or easy times, abundance or scarcity. It didn't address decay. It was what happens to creatures when their environment becomes a joke.

And our reaction became policy.

Decadence is a political response.

Within weeks of starting that party our higher natures became redundant. We would tolerate no delay. The base mood was irritation, broken once a day by the little nirvana of the first hit, which lasted the minutes it took to realise it would only last for minutes. Then spiralling regret, a drowning of sense. But in those highest of minutes in life we grinned and laughed, played music, felt love. It was the feeling promised us by the parents and suits.

But it was our feeling, homemade, from scratch.

Anyway. In the end it wasn't our behaviour that answered any questions, it was the dog. Just as we reacted to the order above us, he reacted to the one above him. A microcosm grew. As we trashed the carpet, he dug up the lawn. We chewed our toys together, became aggressive and unpredictable together. He watched us fall to a place beneath him on the evolutionary scale, without honour or routine. And the more he dug the lawn the more we warned him off. We warned and warned and he dug and dug till one of us finally grew more canine than him. Cesare took to staring him down from the balcony, pinning him into combat with his eyes. Cesare started winning. The dog would slink away beaten, but the matches continued, and grew longer, till one day Cesare jumped roaring from the balcony onto the lawn.

The dog destroyed all the possessions he could find and, the next time the gates were open, fled the house for ever.

Look around the streets and tell me you can't see it happening at large. Everyone staring back, digging holes.

Decadence. The reaction to a chronic joke.

A joke that's always on us.

The party's knell was finally rung by Danny. Who knows if he saw a pattern, made a choice. Who knows who even fucking knew him. But mysteriously, one day, instead of saying 'The moon's a balloon' he said, 'The Pope smokes dope.'

And with that he unfolded his legs, left his bottle, left his home on the floor beside the balcony – and took his red eyes away.

Cesare had stamina, and kept flying until breaking his neck one night at an intersection in his car. He was on his way to score.

The summer rinsed away down a drain, and a part of us rinsed away with it. For ever. It was a summer of forever; nothing we lost there ever came back. Though some time later I saw Danny again, for the last time, on the streets near his house.

He wore a suit, and said we must catch up.

Mechanism

Look at failure. It's like a broken toy, one you can turn in your hands without ever killing the rattle of. It clunks when you pick it up, but doesn't go anywhere anymore.

It looks successful till you get close.

I've turned the thing over a few times, and here's the crux: it's the very idea of a mechanism that makes things fail. A business, a marriage, a life – in conceiving them as mechanisms we wire their failure ourselves. We build structures with blocks bought from parents and peers and concepts from the corners of the press; and build towers from them which fall. As if defining an apparatus will help us deny the real source of triumph: *energy*. There's an aristocracy of those who have failed, and might fail again, but who realise that breezes, winds, and gales of energy are at the heart of all success. We know these people when we meet them. No zealots are among them, no pragmatists nor faint hearts. Determination quietly ripples everything they do. They can feel a breeze on a morning and angle into its stream all day.

One way to find and prove your energy is backgammon. Play it drunk, play it high, play it sober, throw the dice in every mood, before and after good and bad and bent sex; play without cups, feel the dice, warm them in your hand, rattle them, grind them, click them, refuse to play with anyone who uses cups to throw dice. That's where energy will roar. Dice are a quantum translator, an organ of the will, a mirror.

Steal energy if you have to, tell opponents they'll lose, their power will default to you. Play for money, use the cube, frighten yourself. And at the height of a blazing game you'll find that the numbers you call are the numbers you get, you'll see the sparkling source, feel the surge that says you're plugged in.

Energy. Not triumph or defeat. Not luck, nor magic. Just throbbing dark looking for a bulb to light up.

Raise a drink to it, court it.

Be the bulb.

Exodus

I cried when I was baptised. My family doubts me but I can recall it today, despite having been a baby. I cried and cried as my demons left me, or rather stayed back. I couldn't understand the water, I couldn't adjust to the clergy's arms, the echoes through cold shadows, the solemn words.

Years later I had a communion wafer and it tasted bad.

But now the very probable mother of God spoke to me and I was lifted above all baroque and musty history, away from religion's lonely slap. I admit I was taken aback when the phone rang so early. But soon in that twilight of wakefulness, I heard her voice again and remembered how normal, modern and candid human matters become when we can trace them to the flesh they spring from. On this morning I even made her laugh. A great laugh, frothing and full of fun.

'A Nazarene, a Roman, a slave and a donkey walk into a bar,' I said. 'And the barman says: what is this, some kind of joke?'

She laughed and laughed, though it was stupid. My spirits were so high that I made it work, and she let herself be wafted on it, which is the whole glory of silliness. But as my brain woke I wondered if perhaps it was Mary Magdalene after all. She could have been the more receptive to jokes, by reputation at least. In any event, who could tell the nature of either girl by the descriptions handed down to us? There must have been jokes in the minutes of their days, the animals must have done things to cause fits of laughter. There must have been hangovers, flirtations, tantrums, double entendres, misunderstandings and puns. And it's this micro-life which most interests me, it's from these spaces between heroism and tragedy that I feel history's warmth. These were people after all, and between God and destiny there would still be laundry to do. It was in that laundry, in mundane moments that I would glean most from the history of people, whether they became divine or not. And so it was a godsend to crack a bad joke with Mary. I marvelled as she spoke; there she was, in person. All the solemn gospels melted away and suddenly I could understand how divinity could stream like sunlight from one good and candid soul.

It brought another joke to mind: 'A Greek walks into a tailor . . .' I started, but she stopped me, in the nicest way, and said she didn't have much phone credit. Of course, I was being selfish now, just basking in the call. I mean, what a coup for the Church.

'So Mary, I have the euros – if you give me your account details I can transfer them right away.'

'Thank you – but things are worse here, my plans have changed.'

'Oh?'

'Yes, I'm moving away. The place isn't safe anymore.'

'I'm sorry to hear it. Do you need me to book you a hotel? Why don't you take a couple of days out? Get some room service, old movies, and consider everything in a new light.'

The call started to break up. I had to ask her to repeat herself a couple of times. Then it became clear:

'I'm going up to Bethlehem,' she said. 'I met this – guy.'

Well. A pang, I have to admit. Completely misplaced, under the circumstances. Still.

We all know they didn't get up to anything.

'So the cash will be extremely useful,' she said. 'We're so grateful. But would five hundred be too much to ask?'

Fortune

Together we learned about a force beyond confidence.

We tested Fortune.

Lewis had a simple policy: he didn't stop for traffic lights. This was possible in a place where you could buy the law. But added to his other policy of never slowing down, a ride with him made you think. About life, about death; about Fortune. Lewis had Fortune in his pocket – he never wondered, he just knew.

That knowing was it.

We tore up the city day and night in cars. One day I needed a ride. My car was waiting to be collected from a workshop. Lewis came around. A pair of wingmen lounged in the shadows of his car. One was an older, sweetly mellow influence, a soldier with a disability allowance of Quaaludes. A couple of blocks into the drive I realised Lewis had also taken one. His policies were all in place – but his reflexes were out to lunch.

Reaching the intersection where my car sat – we could see it across three lanes of traffic – Lewis hit the gas before the car in front of us was clear. He smacked into the side and bent a panel as it pulled away. There was a pause. His brain scrolled through the usual routines – but slowly. He made no decision until the stricken car pulled over. Then he floored us and shot around the back of the traffic, up the one-way street where my car sat.

Parked cars on both sides of the street only left one lane, but it was a long road and looked clear. Lewis went up it like a stunt driver, until an old Volkswagen beetle nosed around a corner to face us. I remember the driver's face when he saw us – then, edging as far as he could to one side – as he realised we weren't stopping.

Lewis flattened it, aiming for the gap. The car tore panels off the Volkswagen, mirrors and handles off parked cars on both sides. But we made it through. Adrenaline. Lewis's faculties were gone, and even as we prepared to get out and face the music he sped off in a zigzag to the city's ring-road, there to disappear among a million drivers. After putting a safe distance and a good twenty minutes between us and the crimes, he flew through the warrens of a dark, unknown neighbourhood as an added precaution.

Night was falling. We finally coasted to a stop in the shadiest cul-de-sac we could find. Who knows where it was. It didn't matter. Lewis switched off the car. We all lit smokes. But after a few minutes of quiet, marvelling at our escape, we heard the metallic chug of a car, and watched our Volkswagen limp around the corner. The driver stepped out, and after Lewis exchanged insurance details, and the man calmed down – we finally asked the question you ask in a city of 1,500 square kilometres:

How did he find us?

The man pointed to the gate beside our car:

'That's my house.'

Mask

The gas mask was from the sex shop on the high street. Alan rigged it to a hose before drinking himself almost unconscious. To be honest, he thought, it felt more comfortable buying the mask for suicide than for sex. Not that it mattered; the eyes of sex shop attendants are always vacant. Light never burns behind them. Pawnbrokers put themselves across as agents of Right, but sex shop attendants are like strangers in an alley. Personality has fled their bodies so we can be sure they won't judge, or even notice us.

Still, it was one thing that troubled Alan: his last human contact was with a sex shop attendant. At the sex shop. A man with unlit eyes. Sometimes the things we do churn us up, and those ructions lure out the symbols and ironies that Life seems so amused by. Suddenly, all around, like this one, imagine: a sex shop attendant was his last human contact. It's no wonder the world is a mess of pain, if instead of watching over important matters Life is out planting ironies.

Alan lit a last cigarette, setting off in his socks to open the windows – his room mates were non-smokers. Then, to erase the sex shop attendant from the scene, he cleverly thought to call the police. He didn't call the emergency number, but the station, where he imagined things would move more slowly, if at all. The reasoning was that he wanted to be found after death, but before his room mates came home. His body should be found by a professional, someone hard to disgust. They would call other professionals who specialised in the disgusting.

'Police,' a woman answered.

'Hello,' said Alan, 'I'd like to report a dead body.'

'Where are you calling from, Sir?'

'Thirty four Harrogate Road, first floor.'

'Is the body on the premises?'

'Yes it is.'

'Are you the one who found it?'

'Yes.'

'And are you sure the person is deceased? Have you checked for vital signs?'

'Well, I . . .'

'I'll send an ambulance. Is the person known to you?'

Alan thought for a moment, ashing the cigarette into his hand. 'Hang on,' he finally said, 'he seems to be coming round. Yes, yes, he's fine now, thank you.'

Life is no great artist in its designs. Just a decorator. And now the washing machine in the kitchen started to whine, thumping floorboards and rattling dishes in the rack beside the sink. Another symbol. Though Alan had to admit it was he who put the machine on, so as not to leave dirty laundry behind. It was an own goal. The anal are rarely good at suicide. To discover who's good at suicide you need to see who's good in a hotel room; anyone who tidies a hotel room before the maid comes will be a fastidious suicide, with notes and tokens to find, and towels and tape, instead of a lusty expression of blood. As a sensory event the slow spin cycle was a reminder of this. Nothing said more about Alan's life, and about Alan, than the washing machine. It punctuated its slosh and grind with tedious grunts and sighs – then, after an eternity, and for no apparent reason – it spun out.

Do you believe new ZAPPO will get that stain out?

Temple

Music is flavoured air.

Oxygen zest in gusts.

You only have to wait in its draught to feel emotional news from across life, reports on the swell and chop of spirit.

A writer can be driven mad by it. This is no mystery – music doesn't wake till words and meanings are spent. Then it bites the air we breathe, fills the blood stream, spices the heart. A writer pines for this power, gets drunk to forget it.

But, writer: hold back your pen.

Drink from music, cram your veins full.

Then write – smashed on flavoured air.

I came to music from darkness. They were my end times, minefields patrolled by bailiffs and agents of the law. Life's goal was to avoid them. I was a target-rich environment. Nights and weekends were sacred, because agents of that kind tend to have suburban lives, and leave you alone for a while. On weekdays it's different. Sleeping by day is a bad option. Agents are persistent and not easily convinced you're out; sleeping through the night is bad too, as visits outside working hours, early in the morning or long after work, are the most productive in industries built on escapist behaviour. There's only one safe window of time: in the valley between target fields, from ten at night to three in the morning. You have an hour or two of peace before hitting the road and waiting for opportunities to open, in the form of pawnbrokers, betting shops. Dog ends.

This one day was like others at the sharp end of decline. I felt it should be the day I died. I didn't sleep that night, but reflected like a shipwreck on its rocks. The radio accompanied me, and strangely so, because my frame of mind made me switch stations from the usual 'up' programming. I didn't want to hear 'up' anymore. It was a lie. Today compels us to stay up, or if we're uncomfortable there, to at least admit we have a disease of solemnity that can be cured with products and services. But I find that life at the surface becomes black when times are bad, it jeers at you. When things are shit you have to dive. So I found this public radio station offering hushed dialogue between sensitive types, and it was there, this night, that I lost myself in dark thoughts. But then, at some point in the night, the thoughts changed shape; they grew robust, took on edges, became candid. Pains somehow grew sweet, I could touch them as I once toyed with milk-teeth on their last thread of flesh.

What was happening, I realised, was that my feelings were being accompanied. Suddenly they were instruments in a concerto. I sat still on the floor and heard details of my chaos being played by an orchestra. It knew all the havoc, contradiction, confusion, fear – and strode through it all, and out of it all, with purpose. It said that misery was life's default, and asked me to stay close, saying conflict was a human thing, a many-textured set of riddles.

Classical music found me, on the floor. Large orchestras found me there. I took them full in the vein. It was the most direct contact I'd ever had with others who felt the same.

It didn't solve any problems; nights were still short, days were still blighted. But by the time I'd heard Sibelius, Bruckner and Brahms, it mattered less. They hinted at a shore behind the storm.

Notices were served on me to the roller coaster of Britten's piano *Diversions* for left hand alone. A set of Rachmaninov's *Russian Songs* sent me to the phone box to seek help. And as I stayed on the floor, close to these poems of oblivion, life grew inside me again. Big music reformatted my feelings.

I knew all this later when a social worker described to me the contour of an optimal life. It was like the ocean, she said. With one hand she drew a flat line from left to right, and with the other she showed troughs falling under it. Flat was the optimum, she said. It was our job to wipe out the troughs, and just stay flat.

This was the key to a safe and good life.

And just a few weeks earlier I would've agreed.

But suddenly – all these new friends were talking peaks.

Chains

I saw you on the bluff watching humanity gather below. Prophets assembled people across the plains and told them how to reach the promised land, the land of clear air. But it called for sacrifice and labour, I heard them say as I reached you. It called for pain to find that place of freedom. A quiet wind carried these words to the assembly and I watched as the chains were brought out. We had to wear as many as we could, and set off toward the horizon where we would find the land of acceptance.

You and I wandered down because we're nothing if not part of humanity. But when we reached the masses, some people at the edge said stop. You can't come, they said. You haven't earned any chain. You're sceptical and sardonic and cynical and dry and glib. You're not worthy of dragging chain to the promised spot.

Steady on, we said – but no.

Fuck, well. Still, we went along, at a distance, across the prairie, unworthy as we were. A herd is a herd after all. We kept pace and pondered our unworthiness, walking for all the years of our young lives, looking in and watching whorls and helices and blobs form and break apart within the great mass of persons. What we discovered in ourselves was that we believed in people, but that all these people believed in something better still. Something perfect but also invisible, whose only constant was being better; and whose friendship by extension made them better than us.

We didn't so much lack belief in better beings, visible ones, who for instance could turn three hundred tons of metal into an aeroplane – as love them when, having built the plane, they stepped from it dressed as Santa. We liked the astronaut going back into space as an old man – but loved whoever said let's dress up as apes for his return.

People with panache in the face of uncertainty, they were our prophets; not answerers but reminders of spirit. And so, riven from the masses by this tendency, we walked the remaining days, which weren't many because soon, sparkling in the far distance, the tooth-like ridges of the promised land rose up.

Everyone slowed, and we slowed alongside, wondering why; and all at once we saw that between us and the place . . . lay a sea.

And they had earned too much chain to swim with.

Undressing on the beach, we had to look back one last time. Sure, it would be a hard swim; but the sun was on our backs, the weight of our few clothes was left on the sand. And we could see the opposite shore, with its shallows, across the surf. We looked back at the heaving masses, bristling and indignant, clinking and clanking under their loads.

Ciao losers.

How does it feel to have so much chain?

Promise

The island is a dusky flower. Hormones fume in a haze from pavements hot with rain. Sex oozes from mud flats, licks the air sticky, fucks it dead.

Fever.

Butterflies smash on the highways, shards of lingerie blown off the jungle, a shotgun rampage at Frederick's. On an island already toxic with dreams, it calls to the belly pains of love. Take the easterly road into town until the butterflies fall behind. Around a bend towards the stadium: a straight length of harbour. When the flour mill appears to your right, look left. A discrete corner with a sign: 'Caribbean Isle'. Most brothels offer truth, in rubbery flesh, antiseptic air; the fright of fading dreams at night's end. Caribbean Isle offers it. Women strut between lonely tables under light from an ocean floor. Elders dapple a doorway, curry bubbles spices. Stairs creak to speed calypso, Chinese seamen leer at girls Picasso would blame on Goya.

Take care, but not too much.

Soak it up, drink hard.

Then wait.

Surprising things happen at Caribbean Isle.

Promise.

Cox

Driving to work I saw the most beautiful roadkill. It was a carpet of iridescent blue butterflies, squashed but flashing on the highway. Wings twitched and glinted in the heat, making me want to stop and collect them. But under the sparkle were only dead insects. Like suicidal butterflies they swarmed out of the jungle to die under minivans throbbing drum and bass; or when the traffic was light to lie twitching in reggaes that floated down the mountain like fog. Even in death the butterflies were stunning. What a start to a day, to a season, this carpet of beauty and needless death; if any death can be needless, or beautiful. I tried not to run over the things but it was impossible. The drive made me think: whatever gave the creatures their shine in life was still active after death. Beauty survived them, was even framed and made meaningful by death.

I'll never forget them, nor the feelings they inspired.

It was my first day at work on the island. When I arrived at the office I found that a guy lived in the dirt under the building. A young guy, black, with doll's eyes and a jutting lower lip. I discovered he was there when a colleague went to a place on the office floor and jumped on it hard.

'Cox,' he said.

This man shuffled into the office. He was crinkled with sleep, like he'd slept in his clothes. David Cox was his name. His fly was open. He shuffled because his boots had no laces. He took instructions from the colleague for an errand, in a hangdog kind of way, and I noted that his voice lacked the full lilt of Trinidad; instead it had a drawl that tapered to quiet at the end of his words, making them somehow sad. Plus he mushed them in the way of Sean Connery. Cox shuffled away on the errand, probably to find food. I watched his head move past the window, up the road into Port of Spain. Sunbeams smacked the gulf opposite our building, swallowing him up in the gleam. Manatees and mud-crabs must have stirred outside – but it didn't matter if they did, in the languid haze you didn't have to see them to know they were there.

I first came to Trinidad for a cricket match. Now it was my first day at work in an air-conditioned office with a guy living under it. Don't ask me. Granted: I'd had beer, and met fine new comrades. Suddenly I was with them on a Monday morning, not many more than a dozen. They were a sample of the island's blood: Afro-Caribbean, East Indian, Syrian, French Creole, Anglo and Chinese, a culture so bright that my biggest workload wasn't in the office but in local customs and patois, in wining, grining and liming, in doubles, roti and parlour juice, in macajuels, mapipires and pommes cythère, in play whe, soca, chutney and parang. And threaded through it, between a scent of intimate sweat and waiting to hear boa constrictors fall out of trees – I learned more about the guy under the building.

'He fast,' someone said. 'Watch out.'

He presented himself most mornings looking sheepish. Understandable, I thought, if someone jumps around over your sleeping head. Cox was supposedly the building's security guard, though he was absent most of the day, and seemed to roam at night as well. One morning as he shuffled around the office a colleague said there had already been two break-ins during Cox's career – and Cox had committed them both.

I watched his lip drop low in the background.

David Cox had been a street kid before fetching up at the building. At first he'd been allowed to spend his nights indoors; but he was banished outside after something went missing. Our wooden single-storey office was raised off the ground, with a planked skirt around its base that hid the pillars and foundations. The front faced a busy road along the gulf, but at its side was a residential cul-de-sac partly shaded by a coconut palm, and with a ruin across the road that dated back to the coup d'état, now reclaimed by leaves, flowers, and posing herons in the sun; then out back, behind hibiscus and bougainvillea, a dirt corridor ran between the building and the neighbour's fence. Cox had scraped a hole under the planks there, and made a nest of old clothes.

Cox never seemed to wear the same outfit twice. Over time his fashion choices showed that he was a man of drifting spirit – some days he'd appear in an old lady's gardening hat, other days dressed as a pimp, or a child, or a country gent. I was told all his clothes came from a charity bin. He had the biggest wardrobe in Trinidad, and it was also his bed.

'Good morning, Sir, I'll carry your bag,' he'd appear out of nowhere when I arrived in the morning.

'Thanks, Cox, I can carry it. And never mind "Sir", it's only me.'

'Yes, Sir, Mister Sir.'

There was a creeping feeling on the island, like many post-colonial places, that a good turn was a token the bearer expected to redeem one day in cash. With this in mind, and with everything I'd been told about Cox, I tried to keep things cool.

'Sir, Mister Sir, Sir – '

'Cox,' I stopped to face him once. 'You're not my servant.'

'Just testing,' he said.

As weeks passed I saw that Cox was a man on the move, with quick smarts, the wits of a child. As time went on I stayed back later in the office, and as he got used to me being there he would come around. After a while two things would happen at night: at a certain time, late, a shadowy car would pull up outside. Figures would come to the door and hand me foam tubs of food and drink. Cox would show up soon after and claim them. We chatted, he made coffee, used the bathroom. The building's masters didn't want him coming in at night, but he was good with me, and had a good mind. I liked Cox.

'Lend me fifty dollars,' he'd say.

'I'll lend you the sharp end of a pineapple.'

'I was only kidding.'

'The sharp end of a pineapple.'

'What! I was only kidding!'

'Good.'

'But do you have ten? I'll pay you back . . .'

So it went with Cox, who could launch philosophical arguments if you were slow to see his logic.

'Listen to me,' he'd say. 'Have you, in your life, given a total of more than ten dollars to beggars?'

'Of course.'

'But you never saw that money, nor probably the beggars, ever again, right? So here on the one hand you're capable of throwing money clean away – and on the other of resisting to lend to a sort of colleague who you know you'll see every day, and whose life you can make hell until you get paid.'

'Cox – it's a beg. A high-functioning beg because you know I don't want to make your life hell. You're trading on sympathies.'

'What! Do I look like a beggar? Like a man who'd trade on sympathies?'

'Yes.'

'Well. Maybe a technical beg.'

'And don't do the stereotype where I'm rich just because I came from outside, or owe you in a cultural sense because of the colonial past. Everyone has their roll of the dice in life – for now I get paid on the same day as you, by the same people, and until then am in the same condition.'

'Wow. Like you really got out of the wrong side of the bed.'

I look at him.

'Wow,' he shuffles away in his gaping boots. 'Like – at least you *have* a bed. At least you *have* –'

'Cox – I'll give you five dollars. Okay? *Give* them to you.'

'No, no,' he dismisses me over his shoulder. 'Far be it from me to jeopardise the harmony of our interrelationship.' Cox really had a golden tongue, who knows from where.

'Coxy – we're starting to sound like an old married couple. Just take the fiver.'

'Yes, Mister Sir, thank you, Sir.'

'And don't be like that.'

'Okay, but I'll pay you back.'

'You don't have to, that's the idea.'

'But only a *beggar* wouldn't pay it back. Only a *beggar* – '

And so it was, playfully but firmly, that Cox reeled me in. We alternated the roles of mentor and pupil; he with tips from the streets, me with the overworld that was bizarrely out of his reach. For instance, one day he watched me get landed with an extra hour's work after taking a generous stance with a colleague.

'You need to master mood swings,' he sidled up to me. 'Don't be so predictable. Get a reputation for moodiness and nobody will hit on you for favours.' He winked and shuffled away.

Then there was a time Cox started coming in with an old briefcase full of documents. One day he asked if I could read one to him. I wasn't sure if it was because he thought I'd find it interesting – but it turned out he couldn't read or write. He was too shy to ask anyone else. Alongside a small kitchen in the office was a cubby with table and chairs, and Cox would sit there with the briefcase, shuffling papers, furrowing his brow, sighing like a big cheese. Sometimes he'd pace importantly up and down, muttering to himself. You couldn't watch without feeling it in the chest. He had a shine that would have taken him anywhere in life, given only the most basic chances. Instead his energies were turned to grinding small wins on the street. I could relate to Cox. He had some competition in the capital, though: the beggars were the best talkers I'd seen, each with a trademark style. One with a Moses beard, who'd reach out to you like a toddler, whimpering, 'My lord, my lord.' Snappy beggar, who'd sing for a burger; and Fat Beggar, who'd saunter past busy food stalls demanding ten dollars or three breakfasts. Threats as loud as parrots always flocked around Fat Beggar. '*Ten dollars?* I'll crack you down with the door of this car!' Then we had a well-spoken white man who claimed to be Hitler's brother, giving lucid speeches on the fall of the Reich. And there were genuine ragamuffins, who never spoke but scavenged in the gutters of the town; some could only walk on all fours. Where Cox roamed in this sweltering arena, and what he really did, was a mystery to everyone.

One day I scraped through the bushes behind the building to see where he lived. I saw cables running from his burrow, up over the fence into the neighbour's yard.

Cox had cable TV.

I didn't have a TV at home, but Cox had cable. In the dirt. He'd rigged a line from the neighbour's pole. The hibiscus behind the office flickered colours in the night.

Some time after this though, I noticed Cox was more anxious. He was more attentive to his errands, but in a distracted, bumbling way. He forgot about his case of important papers for a time. Then one day I heard his television was gone. He sold it to an old lady, under a sudden crushing debt.

'But how stupid he is,' someone told me. 'He only had it on hire

purchase – who knows how he talked them into it. Now he sold it for less than he owes the shop, and he already spent the money.'

Cox sharpened his wits as this weight bore down. The energy of miracles came to him, as it can to certain people whose pressures blaze persistently inside them. One night, after colleagues finished work, they sent him up the road for a six-pack. Cox went for the beers, came running back with the bottles, but he was careless crossing the avenue, and a car hit him head-on. It tossed him into the air, tossed the beers up over his head.

Everyone watched from the window.

And in the slow-motion reserved for sudden death, we watched him catch the beers on his way back down. Not one hit the deck.

He got up, dusted himself off, and limped to the door.

'Here you go.'

A legend was born in Port of Spain.

But even with the power of miracles upon him – or perhaps because of it – the season wasn't all plain sailing. It saw Cox taking a more vigorous interest in security work, which is a job calling for judgement. Now he called himself 'Chief of Security'. The nights I was there he prowled more noticeably, and came to the door every so often to check on me. He lurked, those days, shifting his gaze around like a spy. He'd be prowling outside when I finished at night, holding up a hand while he scanned the shadows for villains.

This was Cox's spirit the night he spied a man on a nearby rooftop. He got a posse of vagrants together, and with a hail of sticks and rubble they brought the intruder down and bashed him on the ground. But when the police came the man turned out to be the security guard for that building.

The posse vanished into the night, and Cox went to jail. Our bosses didn't bail him out till they'd stopped laughing, which was a full day or two later. After this Cox went back to his sheepish, shuffling self. He came to the office at night with important papers he couldn't read, scrutinising and sorting them with grunts, frowns and sighs. He shaved his head and started wearing these granny-glasses he'd found. Suddenly Doctor Cox, with his glasses, and his case of papers. Not long after this next of his little lives kicked off, I saw him by the avenue with a mobile phone. He paced up and down in earnest conversation, looking this way and that behind his glasses. Cox didn't want to show us his new phone; but I found it one night and it was a rubber toy. One that squeaked when you squeezed it. It also had a little antenna that went up and down.

At his table in the cubby, next to his papers, he sometimes extended the antenna to listen for incoming calls. One time he handled the phone too roughly and it squeaked. He flinched, looking around to see if we'd heard.

After that it stayed in the briefcase.

Everyone reckoned Cox was about twenty-three. He actually carried a birth certificate in his back pocket, and it showed his mother's name. But nobody had put his date of birth.

Cox's mother was long dead.

One night I watched through the window as he sat with a respectable-looking girl. She came from a workplace, in a suit, and Cox met her in dazzling white trousers. They sat on the ledge under the coconut tree. It seemed like a first date. He frowned and smiled and frowned, and his hands framed notions and wonders and surprises for the girl. Occasionally he stepped away to take a call on his phone. I lurked behind the window praying it didn't squeak.

As I began to lock up that night, Cox rushed to meet me on the steps. When he was nervous or frightened his eyes grew round, and he clenched his teeth so you could see them clenched. I didn't want to make eye contact, I knew his position; all he felt he could offer the girl was a pantomime of worth, a first date on a ledge under a tree. I wondered if maybe that's all any of us can offer.

'Mister Sir, Sir . . .'

'Don't worry,' I said. And as I passed the girl, 'See you tomorrow Doctor Cox.'

The girl didn't come around again. I suspect she might have liked to; but Cox only had the ledge under the coconut tree to entertain her. He'd illuminated what might have been, and that was all he felt he could offer. Plus eventually the phone would've squeaked.

He went back to his paperwork at night, shuffling and sorting it in and out of his case. He used to ask if I had any official-looking papers I could add to his collection, and I gave him some bank statements and bills. But after reading the occasional letter for Cox I started noticing some were addressed to him. They were from businesses and civic groups; statements of support for a charity.

Cox had started a charity. With his glasses and briefcase, and maybe his phone, he'd been trawling the town raising support for a children's charity. A charity for kids like him. Businesses were offering to host bins on their premises where people could leave Christmas gifts. Then at Christmas Cox would deliver the gifts to poor children and orphans. The image brought howls of laughter in our building. Hilarious speculation as to how Cox would fit all the toys in his burrow, and where he would fence them for cash; but then came a shout from the directors' office. We crowded at the door, where we could see his TV – and there was Cox.

Cox was on TV with Miss Universe.

Trinidad & Tobago with her neighbour Venezuela have more than a fair share of Miss Worlds and Miss Universes; one of the most recent to that time was Trinidadian. There she was with Cox. He wore his glasses. They laughed together. Later that day he passed by the office to a hail of jeers, taking a bow before going out to find whores for some Chinese seamen off a rusty freighter. Later he stole coconuts from the office tree, was discovered, punished, and retired to his hole under the building.

That was Cox's day in the sun.

When Christmas came the office turned into a distribution centre for gifts. Things looked up for Cox, for a while at least. Then he rattled the door one night and asked if he could use the phone. I let him in, paying no attention to his call. But strangely for the time of night, a second line started ringing. I took it on another phone and it was the boss calling from home. He wanted to know how Cox was using the office phone.

Cox had called a live radio phone-in and accused a government minister of being a racist. The boss was listening to the show. That ended Cox's nights in the office. His timing could've been worse though; carnival season approached, and the island soon became a whirl. Carnival was prime season for Cox and the beggars, the place filled with strangers, streets were awash with flesh, beer and rum. Occasionally his face would appear like a light-bulb here or there around town – at the back of a party, on a carnival float, running with tourists. Afterwards, Carnival hangover seemed to last months. The office was slow to cure.

When I next saw Cox he had mange growing on his skin, and lumps in his neck. The mysterious car still delivered food most

nights, but now it went mostly uneaten. I ate some, I confess.

I soon heard Cox had AIDS.

He'd met a tourist one carnival a few years earlier, as a teen. They ended up at the tourist's hotel. I never found out if the tourist was male or female, if the sex was consensual, or sold. When you knew Cox, it was as fucked-up an idea as a child abduction. Cox wasn't a waster, he wasn't a druggie, he wasn't true street crew. Hell, he giggled like a little girl the night we goaded him into half a bottle of beer.

He knew things were uncertain. Apparently his HIV was diagnosed years before. Now it was full-blown AIDS. Everyone had kind of known; they just let me figure it out for myself.

Our boss was a cool and clear-hearted man. He made no big deal of Cox's ups and downs, he bantered and sparred with him as much as he ever had; but there were doctors in his family, and through him Cox was treated for free all those years.

Now his lip hung lower than ever. He started to dribble. He started to lose his height and build. His skin lost its shine. Even so he'd rally from time to time, young Doctor Cox would emerge with his spectacles and his crucial business dealings.

But Cox knew he was sick.

One night he asked if I thought there was anything after death. I told him plenty of intelligent people think so.

The shadowy car that delivered his supper turned out to be from one of the finest restaurants in town, not far around the corner. The pair of formidable women who ran it had been reeled in like the rest of us. As Cox slowed down and grew more dazed, as the glands on his neck swelled, and his body showed its bones, these connections in his life quietly appeared.

One day Cox was rushed to Accident and Emergency. My colleague Kirtlee and I put on ties and strode into Port of Spain General Hospital to find him. He was on a big ward.

'It's nothing,' he said, 'just a cough. Tell them I'm coming back.' And he did come back for a while. But he soon disappeared again.

This time it was to a place on a mountainside with a view over jungles. A misty place where bird cries echoed. It felt like a place you didn't come back from. I had to leave the island for a few weeks and before I left I made the trip to find him. He was on a bed next to a prisoner in chains. He spread out his hands and grinned with clenched teeth at the colossal joke of it all.

'I'm dying,' he said.

It was a scrape his wits couldn't help him out of. I brought him food, and a wallet stuffed with official papers for his collection. But seeing him there wide-eyed I knew his spirit had flowered and shrunk away, his time had come and gone. I hugged him, and told him to wait for me, I'd bring him something back from my travels.

But Cox couldn't wait.

He told his last visitors I was coming back. But I heard on the phone from them that he was dead. They buried him in Lapeyrouse cemetery, on his home patch near the office. His friends came from the building, the restaurant, and an unexpected number out of the woodwork of gingerbread houses, palms and shadows.

I don't know if Miss Universe was there.

By then it didn't matter.

Mist hung over Port of Spain when I got back. It was butterfly season again. The highway was spattered with needless victims.

They hadn't lived long.

But they flashed fire and colour from where they lay.

Lizards

Don't drink with lizards at New Year.

I tried it, big mistake. Though perhaps they were agents of change in the long run. Change of mind. Everything lives inside an idea, that's the thing. Pineapple is a word that contains a pineapple, making the word itself prickly and sweet.

I grew bored with New Year. Or maybe just new. Or year. I started to find that there were no years. All we did was punctuate time at random. Party-poppers didn't make anything new.

New Year lost all meaning.

I had to make a decision. It was to leave the party-popper arena, where this sad finding arose. I told everyone I wouldn't be coming for party-poppers. Then I bumped into old friends in front of the surgical bootmaker's shop. Old school mates that included Werner Niedermayer the bully. He was still a cunt, but he invited me to his New Year's party. Might be a laugh I thought.

Anyway, lizards.

My advice is don't drink with them. One minute you'll be there, with a drink in one hand, touching a lizard with the other – next thing you know, you'll turn around and just the lizard's tail will be left. You turn around for a hug, to say Happy New Year – and the lizard's body will be gone. Bang. Just like that. Then you're just left with this empty tail.

I'm not saying it's an accident. Lizards can jettison their tails. Just like that. You just have to bury it, I suppose.

Who knows what you tell the other guests.

Don't drink with snakes at New Year either.

I tried it, fuck that for a game.

One minute you're there, with a drink in one hand, your arm softly around a large snake. Next thing you know, you're still there, but somehow, from inside, the snake has just gone and left its skin.

Snakes. Never trust them.

They just leave their skins.

You end up having to pretend it's a wind ornament or something, which can make you look like a hippie. You may as well wear beads as try passing off empty snakeskin to the other guests.

One year, though, I got so drunk that when I looked around I was the one with a tail. I glanced once, quickly, and just kept making conversation, in case the others noticed. I went to the bathroom later and it was there. I could've died. I stuffed it down a trouser leg but it didn't really work, the tip poked out.

Imagine my relief when I stepped out and saw other tails in the crowd. Werner Niedermayer had one. *Werner Niedermayer*. And that Gisela girl had one, a white skinny one. It had the same sheen as her skin, and sagged a little on the carpet. I couldn't help wondering exactly where it was attached. I nearly stepped on it. She flicked it behind her with a sexy little thrust of her hips. I was impressed. We never got off that night, but I kept thinking about running a hand up her tail till she quivered.

One year some tequila appeared around eight o'clock. Next thing I knew, must have been around midnight or so, I stepped aside to let a guest pass me in the hall, and my whole skin stayed behind. I could've died. Then someone brushed it with a cigarette, sending this evil smoke into the kitchen. Chips and dip were delayed, and quite a few people knew why.

Imagine my relief when I got to the bathroom and saw two more collapsed skins against the laundry basket. I could swear one was Niedermayer. *Werner Niedermayer*.

All collapsed and empty.

Anyway, tequila. But when I came back into the party I saw Niedermayer splayed across the sofa, all shiny and new, with women each side of him. It was like a deodorant commercial, because everyone was looking at him with sparkling eyes, and he was growing fat on the attention.

For fuck's sake, Niedermayer.

What he was saying, if I remember correctly, after all those tequilas, was that a New Year's party wasn't about New Year at all. It was about Old Year. I think that's what he said. *Old* Year. Everyone shone when he said this. I saw another fresh skin over by the speakers where this pumping dance vibe was happening, wobbling it around. You could've danced with it.

Old Year was the key to the party, apparently. After a hard year certain people can wield conceptual control over their body mass. All the stresses and drawbacks of a year could be secluded in a tail, or in the skin. The code of all their mistakes could be allocated to these things, filed there, and after midnight on January the first they could simply shed them and start again.

This was all meant to happen conceptually.

For fuck's sake, Niedermayer, I was reaching for another drink by this stage. I felt like asking where this left the Chinese, who don't even have a January the first.

'Oh, Werner,' everyone said.

I felt like asking how the same bad karma in a tail, which in his case could weigh upwards of ten pounds, could also be stored in the skin, which was so light that it collapsed like an empty condom. Surely some math missing there.

'Oh, Werner.'

This year we have a tropical theme. Who knows what they put in the punch because I'm already on the floor. I'm not only on the floor but it's as if I'm blind. It's as if I'm trapped in a ball of hard wool, and blind. Just waiting for someone to ash their cigarette and send me up in flames. I could die.

I can't even find my drink.

I scratch a hole in the wool and it opens quite easily. I find that I'm not blind – I'm just wrapped in a hard woollen thing. I roll it left a little, and wouldn't you know it: over by the sofa is another woollen torpedo, and Werner Niedermayer is climbing out of it. He's all sticky, like he honked on himself. He probably did, who knows what they put in the punch.

Then, oh my God – when he gets up these kind of sheets unfold off his back. They thwack open, twitching, and everyone jumps.

They're *wings*.

'Oh Werner!' everyone cries.

One of the guests is laughing hysterically, I think that redhead from the Italian place up by the bridge, and throws open the French windows. Big hit of cold pours in.

By this time I have both arms out. Frankly I'm reaching for another drink. But when I look back up, I see Niedermayer swaying at the windows. He takes a deep breath. Then he flies away over the balcony and up into the night.

'Happy New Year, Niedermayer,' I shout after him.

Typical, he doesn't hear me. I can't even see him anymore.

I'll have to go after him, he's drunk.

My wings unfold, the redhead strokes one and gets dust on her hand. She says it's her first year at the party. As I steady myself on the balcony I leave her a word of advice: don't drink with lizards.

Wait for butterflies instead.

Then I take flight over the rooftops. 'Werner!'

He's still such a cunt.

Relax, they're only concepts

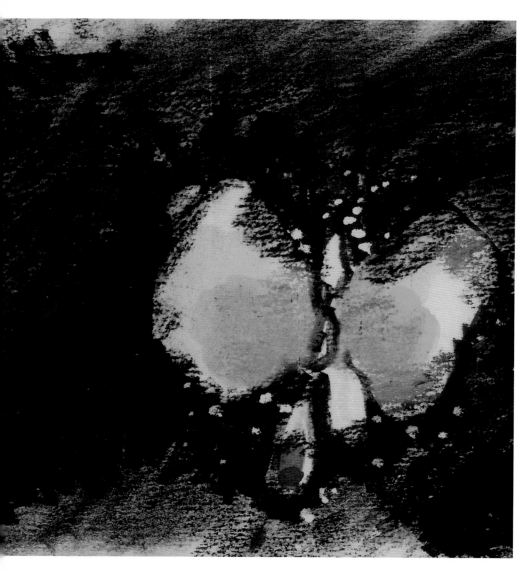

Lust

In my room there's a woman I can't see or speak to. But I can taste her. Taste her coming my way. I entice her with my mind, scrape a clearing on its floor for her to blare like brass music.

My chutney bacchanal.

My sin, she poisons me slowly, insufficiently. So I love her. To possess her I've only to make sounds with my mouth. The gasps, the stings we'd enjoy if only I spoke, but I don't, can't speak to her at all. So I pelt kernels of aching smut hoping one will explode.

I'll fill her with my fury.

She knows it. She feels me call to her.

And I know she'll come to me. In time.

So here you find me. My life of carefully matched socks, awkwardness with family, goal-setting ideals, is reduced to this throbbing thing. No plan but to live like a worm in her nectar.

She's close. I sense her bend forward beside me, an oyster bed in silk, a taste of nuts chewed with butter burnt in blood.

Then footsteps. Now voices.

'Are they ready?' asks a man.

'As they'll ever be, I suppose,' says my girl.

'Sort out that hose, can you? Pressure's all over the place.'

The routine is different today. I don't know why. I don't dwell on it either, being more concerned with her air of detachment. I ache with her detachment. Her voice gives no hint of this fever. Instead she slides tidily around the room, not moaning my name but serving words as ordinary as cups of tea. Wasted little trout. She always plays this way. She moves lightly, sometimes singing softly and tunelessly, always Top Ten. It drives me insane. She's life itself. I rage to reach out and smack her with the flat of my hand.

But I can't.

'Signatures?' the man asks from the door.

'Uh-huh,' she says.

'All yours then. Let me know if you need a hand.'

'Thanks, I'll be fine.'

She'll be fine. She'll be fine when I suck the womb out of her. I track the man's steps as they move away up the corridor.

Then we're alone.

She moves closer. Her breath overwhelms me, her sleeves blow scent across my face. This is a liberal if not bohemian young woman who's baked a conservative crust around her steaming drives and delights in the effect of their vapours escaping. My pheromone barb. Her breath blows me pictures of her drenched in wild sobs.

I hear her thighs. Actually hear them softly meet as she leans over to prise open one eyelid, then the other, even though she knows the game by now. I see her clearly, even with my eyes shut. I'll have her just now, take her by the scruff with my teeth and slam her like a frenzied dog. As she leans close I beg one of my hands to fly to her, cup her before she can blush. But no hand obeys, save the hand of my mind, or perhaps it's my soul, this blazing rag.

Another voice through the door: 'Do you want them now?'

'Give me a minute. I'll tidy him up.'

The tips of her fingers flick through what's left of my hair. She straightens the sheet across my chest, smooths it with the flat of her hand. Then a wet flannel scrapes over my face like a mother's tongue. My body lays quiet, but I can't stop the dream where my soul arches glistening above the bed, crackling with shock, parting her legs like halves of a wishbone. Soft as air the fingers of my soul grow tentacles; but I feel nothing.

Feet shuffle through the door. Familiar perfumes approach.

A sob pops over me.

'Will he feel anything?'

It's my wife. Her voice is strained and comes with the tinkle of forty-three charms on a bracelet made of years I assured her were golden. My son shuffles beside her, a sensible man, charged like all children with dismantling a net of family lies.

'He won't feel a thing,' says Nurse, 'you can be sure of that.'

'But I read somewhere that they can still hear, and think.'

Nurse hesitates. 'Although it's unpleasant, this is quite routine. Our best knowledge is that his reception of stimulus won't change.'

There's a pause. I feel another hand on my forehead; my wife's.

Nurse steps to her side. 'I'm sorry. It might help if you accept that the person you knew has already passed away. He hasn't responded to stimuli in over a week. I assure you his vital signs will go within a minute of being unplugged. We've done all we can.'

'He had a good innings,' says my son. And to the nurse, 'Thank you, we don't need to see any more.'

'Let me walk you back to the lounge. Doctor Bowman would like to see you, and I'm sure we can arrange some tea or coffee.'

As their footsteps recede, my soul stiffens with the guilty resolve of a nine-year-old. Throbbing flanges erupt from my body with a screech, dirty wings with arteries and organs unfurl like petals to gather and twist around a smoking tower of flesh already in spasm.

Nurse's footsteps approach.

I wait quiet, alone, between life and death.

Rabid with them both.

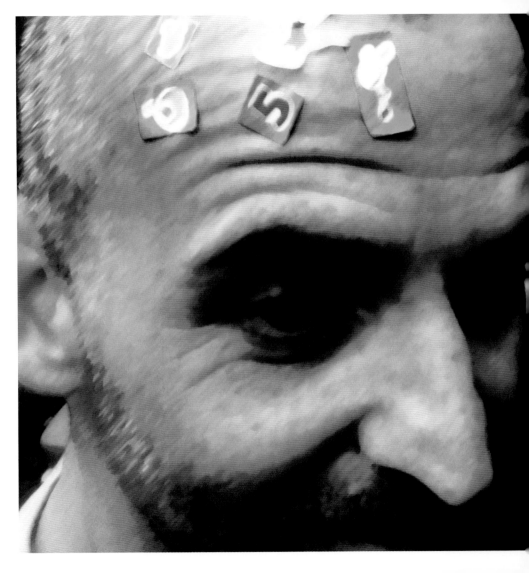

Foot

'Hello, hello,' I tie the robe, shuffling to let her in. 'I was just going to shower.'

Odille steps in, looking around. 'Wow. Are you okay?'

Suggestion is a powerful thing, and as she asks I feel the entrance swim around me. Throwing back my head makes it spin even more. My knees start to buckle. She jumps to steady me, hands hot and firm, and leads me to the bed where she lets me fall. She frowns the frown of someone rebuking themselves for hoping.

'Water,' she says, gliding to the bathroom. Then: 'What! It's a massacre in here!'

Moments of quiet follow. I hear a sniffle. She comes to stand at the end of the bed, looking down at me.

Her chirp is gone. Her flounce is gone.

'Sorry,' I croak, trying to reach the phone without lifting my head. Salty blood runs down my throat, and the backwash that escapes into my mouth makes my teeth click when they touch. 'I'll order coffee. Sorry, sorry. But there's a good reason, I assure you. I'll get some coffee and pain au chocolat.'

She snatches up the room-service menu. 'What! Continental breakfast is thirty euros! Are you crazy? What are you even doing here? Every time I see you it's a different nightmare!'

'Nightmare? Well. But the breakfast will be very good.'

She tosses down the card. 'I don't need anything. Thank you.'

Something in me decides this is the moment to explain the effect she has on me. But as I start out, a cough sends a thread of blood flying through my lips. It sails out to the end of its shiny tether before slapping back onto my chin. I glance at her.

'If you can pay for this, you can pay for a doctor.'

I suck back some blood and watch her reach for the phone, full stretch across the bed. 'Don't need a doctor,' I say. 'I'll shower.'

'You think I can walk out and leave a man spitting blood?' She dials reception. 'You're too scary.' Her phone voice is precise and cordial. Charming, the voice of *petite Madame*. Twisting onto her belly, drawing up a knee, she lights the suite up. I'm on a bed with her, and even bet I can feel her warmth.

I move a hand closer.

She suddenly sits up. A buttock grazes my hand, I recoil.

'Ah – is that what you want!' She leaps off the bed. 'What – you think what! Because of my bad foot you think I'll do anything? And be grateful? Is that it?'

'No, no – ' I try to sit up.

'A stranger did the same to me once – and it felt like this! *It felt just like this*! Because someone thought I was crippled, and could take any amount of damage, even be grateful that he touch me!'

'I don't think you're crippled! No!'

'I come here like a friend and you violate me on a bed! Ah – now it's all clear! You phone me drunk already, sick already! I'm a prostitute, right? I have a bad foot so you don't even have to invite me for dinner! You just call for the last fuck!'

'Odille! No!'

'I was abused and then you call me a prostitute!'

'No, no!' my eyes swell. 'No – and I was abused too! I was abused too, as a child!'

'I have a bent foot, and I was abused – and then you say I'm a prostitute!'

'No! Well – I have scars too! Odille? We're both victims!'

'And then you call me a prostitute!'

'No! Well – ' I'm beaten on that one point.

'My foot makes me so worthless that I'll be grateful, is that it? I'll ignore the fact that you're a stinking, bleeding, disintegrating man, and just fuck you for some Louis XV décor!'

And there the point returns to me.

I sit up with the vain comfort of the righteous.

It is of course Louis XVI.

Bomb

This girl left me at Christmas. A whiff of shampoo stayed back, unexploded. 'We Three Sirens', 'Silent Siren', 'Red-nosed Siren', these imbeciles came singing in the road, strafed my halls with smears of siren. The only comforts around were a taste of old lipstick, jingling lies and pine-needle smells.

Visceral. It was life but the live red cable of it, the naked, sparking end. I made an amulet and stuck it to my belly to bring her back. I don't know why my belly. I'd had brandy. Tied with threads of her clothes, the amulet was an external organ, a plug-in heart, a fuse and a detonator. All the longing could focus there while I survived. I could roll it in my hand and know it was the pain, the hope and the way. The nugget stuck to me day and night, even survived swimming. Then one night I missed its prickle. It was during a party. It fell off into the lawn and was gone. And after searching a few times, once I was convinced of never seeing it again – the pain went away.

Before the next screening of *A King Is Born* I moved from that address forever. The amulet is still there.

If you occupy that house, never touch it.

Delinquent

Prepare for another dark page in the catalogue of global security failures. One against which there aren't enough police in the land.

An elderly and obese Caucasian male remains at large, suspected of going equipped to enter, and actually entering, domestic premises in hours of darkness for the purpose of influencing minors. Such is the man's hold over his vulnerable prey that none break their silence. The suspect is a non-resident foreign national of ambiguous provenance who ignores legal ports of entry. Given his age and body mass he could easily fall ill in this country, placing yet another burden on struggling health services. Further, the suspect is known to have had contact with undocumented livestock prior to entering the country; in fact he is an importer of alien livestock, in flagrant breach of quarantine laws, and a patent threat to an already decimated farming industry. This ostensibly self-employed manufacturer exploits an unpaid special needs workforce. He imports vast numbers of children's durables with small parts potentially hazardous to infants, as well as controversial entertainment devices widely linked to aggressive pathologies, rampant obesity, sloth, ill manners, and attention deficit among an entire generation of young.

Behavioural profiling points to a substance abuser, as theft and disposal of foodstuffs frequently feature at the scenes of his crimes. His body weight seems to bear this out. And he is further in commission of numerous and grave breaches of aviation law, as well as repeated acts of cruelty to animals, most notably in forcing numbers of Eurasian reindeer to circumnavigate the globe by air in a single night, without lights, navigation equipment, or accepted aeronautical registration, and with scant regard for members of the public beneath their flight path.

The profile is alarming. Yet despite many sightings over the years not much is really known about this serial offender. Facial hair forms part of the profile, though any defensive psychologies or religious attachments behind this remain obscure; he is rumoured to have a partner by marriage, though no confirmation has ever entered the public domain, neither any suggestion the union has been genetically fruitful.

Although in a very real sense 2.5 billion people can't be wrong – I really wonder about this Nordic serial trespasser. The world has a circumference of over 21,000 nautical miles. This suggests to me that claims he offends against every victim on the same night are at best exaggerated. And while, consistent with others of his type, his abuse masquerades as generosity, still a majority of his target victims – supposedly numbering every child in the world – are without a toy, his primary tool and chilling calling card.

Such are the discrepancies that I wonder if the Nordic serial offender is a myth put out in bourgeois cultures to cause insecurity – and thereby, public order and shopping. The signs are compelling. Just compare these ten points against the best-known terrorists:

1   His character is defined, but not well defined.
2   He's stereotyped, even uniformed, so we can spot him.
3   He doesn't age.
4   He reproduces himself in greater numbers every year.
5   His occurrence is widely foretold in the media.
6   He speaks occasionally from an implausible location.
7   He never fails to occur when predicted.
8   A majority of the population undergoes significant inconvenience and alarm preparing for his arrival.
9   The country's airports cease to function.
10   He laughs at us, and is *never* caught.

Binoculars

We decided to become American businessmen. This lasted until our first product failed, which was a week. The product was middle-class binoculars: a pair of spectacles with a curtain-rod glued to the top of the frame, and little net curtains that hung over the face. Perfect for Christmas. In this way the middle classes could practise the same insecurities on the street as they enjoyed at home. But here we hit the wall of global commerce: Americans don't do net curtains. We also hit our first philosophical problem, and a realisation that society didn't see things as we did: in the minds of some people, you couldn't be middle class to promote the binoculars; plus we were foreign and hence exempt from class struggle, particularly the middle one which struggles both ways. For some people this erased the joke and unique selling point of the binoculars, though obviously they still carried a principal benefit, which was privacy in the public domain. According to some people, the concept would only be perfect when marketed from within the class structure.

For us this was wrong thinking, but anyway.

We decided to just be Americans.

At this time.

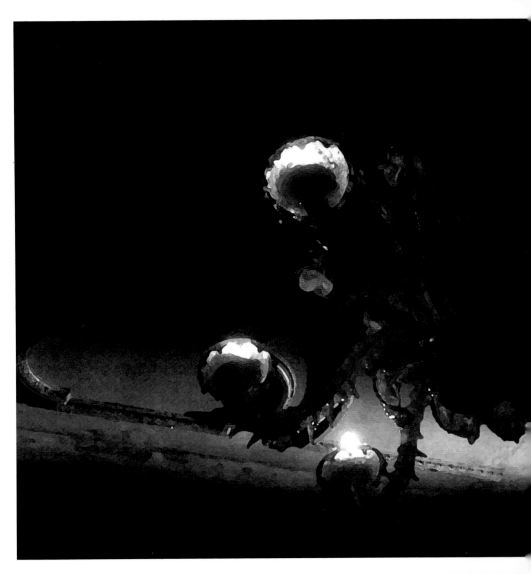

Soho

Morning breaks last in Soho. She sails in the evening to the farthest place you can go. When she returns at dawn grimy shadows flee back to abnormal down her planks. A galleon of wood and rope whose timbers creak an opera of denizens opening their sails. Her guns are made of dark, her raveners, ravers and rovers are blown by hot gales. Fragments of thought travel her rigging and collide as ideas of universal significance for only that moment. Down near the floor is where they scoot, on their way to the moist pan of London to be rinsed into nonsense. London is wet, Soho is dry. A fertile mind gets gritty in Soho from winds as they eddy around corners.

The appropriate is inappropriate in Soho. The girl thinks she has a peace sign tattoo but it's a Benz logo, one of the bars is missing. As she watches to see if a tramp in a doorway is alive, his phone rings in his pocket and he wakes to tell her the air smells of vanilla, another sign the world will end. A big coloured thought flaps through the air from the west, that distant trains always sound like pain. It peters out near the corner of Dean Street and dies there.

No trains come to Soho.

Soho is out till further notice, there's nowhere for a train to come. She's out on high seas, fuck off. There are cities and neighbourhoods inside cities where locals can be cast as horrified victims in films where monsters rise out of the sea to threaten them. Not Soho. No monsters rise there. No monsters, no victims, no captains on a bridge. She's the monster, we her catamites. Our love is pure because we're not in charge and nobody is in charge. The reality is that it's a dream world and the dream is that her heaving through the night under our feet is real.

In Soho our quest for meaning may prove to have no meaning; but it won't have a meaning we disapprove of.

Anyway who cares. Fuck off.

Till tonight.

X-mas

The phone is buried on the other side of the bed. I'm aware of things flying to the floor as I reach for it. It's Christmas but still a brutal hour to call. Likely suspects scroll through my brain – then I hear a donkey bray through the earpiece, followed by a girl's voice.

It's the probable mother of God.

I must find it out for sure.

I hear her send someone away with the donkey. Then she says: 'It's terrible of me to ask – but is your offer of a hotel still open?'

'What's happening, Mary?'

'My friend didn't book anywhere and now we're in Bethlehem with nowhere to stay. The place is full. Who knows what we'll do.'

'Uh-huh – but if everywhere's booked then I might not have any more luck on the net.'

The signs were adding up: donkey, Bethlehem, Christmas.

I know our Christmas wasn't His birthday, but this odyssey's timeline is rubbery beyond the scale of that error, and in a way I don't have the maths for.

'Plus I don't feel well,' says Mary. 'I picked up a stomach ache.'

And there you go.

'We passed a Crowne Plaza at Jerusalem,' she says, 'I didn't try it because of the donkey. But maybe if we had a booking . . .?'

I sit up. It all becomes clear. This early morning a fulcrum of history falls among the bedsheets. The weight of two thousand years presses down. One wrong move and – who knows what.

Things have been headed this way. And now they're here.

I was called upon to act.

'Crowne Plaza, eh?'

I could do it on Priority Club points.

Or I could pay, and *earn* Priority Club points.

I could earn Priority Club points off the birth of God.

Which you'd have to think would parlay into Platinum Ambassador status, somewhere down the line.

Christ could be born in a deluxe King with complimentary Wi-Fi and a welcome gift. It all makes perfect sense.

But then it doesn't.

Hypo-allergenic pillows. Molton Brown amenities.

I picture the Nativity.

Kings in the lobby.

Camels by the shuttle.

Club sandwich crusts on a room-service tray by the door.

O Holy crusts.

I picture the school play of it.

The greeting card.

Typical for it to fall to me at Christmas. Suddenly the Christmas without the girl was easier. I light a cigarette, and consider it all very seriously. After all, surrealism aside, a young couple is facing a night on the streets, or worse – in a stable.

'Mary,' I finally say. 'I've thought hard about this, and felt it with my heart – and I'm just not sure Crowne Plaza is what you need for tonight. There are just things you may not know.'

'Oh,' she says. 'Well – that's a shame. My friend brought a camera. I could've given you a password for my channel.'

'Booking it now – name of Magdalene.'

News

It's ten o'clock. Two more mainland airports closed to inbound flights this morning as the army entered its fourth day of manually screening stranded passengers. In one instance fifteen hundred people were trapped in a tunnel between Heathrow Terminals One and Three when screening equipment in both terminals failed, causing the tunnel to be sealed. The equipment's manufacturer says it's working around the clock to resolve sensitivity issues with the scanners, all of which failed after detecting residual laser-tag codes on passengers and staff involved in clearance sales earlier in the month. The cutaneous tags had proved popular during the sales season as a way of avoiding contact with goods, and were being touted as the answer to the season's rising death toll. Mortality figures for this year's sales remain provisional, with a full count expected by April. Your community mentor advises that it's safer to shop at home and pay the difference.

All non-essential travel is forbidden today under emergency powers. Anyone venturing out can expect limited access to rail, air and ferry hubs, as well as lengthy screening by curfew officers.

The trail of eco-fugitive Carlos Damiana has gone cold near Avignon in France, where Special Branch officers joined Interpol and local police in a house-to-house search today. Damiana escaped custody just hours before his extradition to the United States on charges connected to his role in the October bombing of the Insurance Arm building, which resulted in the deaths of thirty-eight people, one of them an American national. Your community mentor reminds you to be terrorist aware – it could be a neighbour.

A new study published today in the journal of science sheds definitive light on the relationship between humans and climbing. The study's authors claim it shows no evidence linking human instinct with the urge to climb objects over a metre high, stating instead that this relatively recent habit developed through what they call 'Ape bias' – an over-identification with historical theories linking humans to the evolution of apes. Any tendency among today's young to want to climb, they say, is simply bad parenting, and a hangover of those now disproven theories. 'Apes climb,' they say. 'Humans sit down.' Your community mentor warns that apes display violent habits which we should in no way identify with.

A New York man is set to bring a forty-billion-dollar defamation case against the United States government for persistently referring to him as 'Mister' in their correspondence. Jackson Wiese claims the title is segregationist and oppressive under current human rights legislation, saying he first warned the government against the title's use in 2030, and that their failure to respect his individual rights since then constitutes deliberate and malicious persecution. Your community mentor advises you to let strangers originate contact through a symbol pad.

Finally, an eleventh-hour twist in the case of radical female-rights campaigner Lisa B. has resulted in a hung electronic jury at the virtual Old Bailey. A widespread system failure, possibly linked to residual shopping tags, may have misplaced or even deleted the files containing images of the campaigner wearing a skirt, which formed the basis of the prosecution's case. A court spokesperson says unless the files can be produced this week, Person B. may have to be released pending further inquiries. Your community mentor advises you to remain gender-offender aware – it could be a neighbour.

Due to today's emergency powers, there is no weather.

Key

A billion stories like this one unfold every hour, but it's unusual to see one whole – which is what the story's about. When political scientist Louis Halle joined the US State Department after the Second World War, he was already interested in the difference between what is taught and what is practised in international relations and in life. Early on he attended a lecture by a senior State Department official on how policy was made. The Secretary of State's office was the tip of a pyramid, the official said, and policies flowed down through ever more specialised departments towards implementation. The lecture and the process it explained – policies at the top, implementation at the bottom – were elegant, and the attendees, including Halle, were heartened.

But Halle saw something different. To begin to explain what he discovered about people and their endeavours, he recorded the following example; to his knowledge he was the only one who did.

A routine message arrived from an assistant speech-writer at the White House. It asked the State Department to send proposals for President Truman's inaugural address the following January. State Department staff got together and proposed three points: a statement in support of the United Nations; a confirmation that the European Development Programme would continue; and an intention to set up a defence treaty between Atlantic allies.

When the group was asked for any more ideas, one official recalled an informal conversation he'd had about the country's technical assistance program to Latin America – could they say it might extend to other regions?

Without discussion the idea went down as Point Four, and the meeting ended. Then, as that list rose through State Department hierarchy on its way back to the White House, Point Four was discarded. It would be; it had no reason, no background, no plan – it was a throw-away. So only three points made it to the president's office. But days later the department got a call from that office: the three points were okay as fillers – but was there something more original the president could say? The man who answered the call thought for a moment – a fourth point had been rejected, he said.

Point Four went back on the list.

Point Four was a public relations gimmick thrown in by an assistant speech-writer on the phone, according to Halle. Nothing more was heard of it until the speech.

The day after the speech it was seized on as a headline by the press. The White House and State Department were broadsided. Nobody knew anything more about Point Four than was in the speech – there were no answers for journalists, no outlines for congress, no briefings for diplomats. It was a conversation. A policy that travelled from bottom to top. Things didn't happen that way.

Point Four entered the press as a 'Bold new program', forcing the White House to start making plans. According to Halle it took twenty-one months of confusion, breaking the backs and careers of many good people, to put anything resembling that program into effect. But into effect it went, becoming what is now the *Agency for International Development*, a keystone of foreign policy.

At a press conference six days after the speech, the president was asked to give some background on the origin of Point Four.

He said:

The origin of Point Four has been in my mind, and in the minds of the government, for the past two or three years, ever since the Marshall Plan was inaugurated. It originated with the Greece and Turkey propositions. Been studying it ever since. I spend most of my time going over to that globe back there, trying to figure out ways to make peace in the world.

The punchline: he wasn't lying.

The spirit of Point Four was in the air at the time; it just needed someone to claim the accident and engineer it into history. This, Halle discovered, is what people do. He had access to a torrent of diplomatic memos pouring in and out of his department and, on comparing what people think happens with what actually happens, he decided that our times are largely made of accidents upon accidents. He could teach how things were meant to happen, but not how they happened, because every accident is different.

It's down to people. The more chaos we find, the more earnestly our brains write dramatic fiction – smooth, rational progressions from A to B, where we're purposefully in charge, where we're even heroic. It's why a big lie works better than a small one: the mind works that much harder to make it real. We chaperone it.

And so to writing.

Fiction works because we practise it every day. We write our lives while accidents write us, linking, honing, dramatising every minute, using all the tools of the novelist. We're not just hungry, we could 'eat a horse', we don't just party, we 'get mortal'. We attach motive and reason and drama to uncontrollable chaos. It's why we can put ourselves in a character's shoes – he also lives in a fiction. And I like the form, it's fun.

But it's legend. Accident is real.

I'm very conscious of life in these two worlds. But now our legends have been hijacked, the gap between worlds has grown so wide, jimmied by commerce with government on its heels, that we've become edgy. What we hear and what we see don't match.

We have to work too hard to rationalise the stories and offers. To me it says that we should pick a world and climb aboard. Give up weaving them together.

So I started romancing chaos.

Up to now, when my writing gets kicked, it's often over Form. But the more I taste life beneath the legends, the more I sense truth is a play between accident and nature with legends dragged behind it. It explains all irony. It makes a reggae of everything we believe runs like clockwork – and I've tried to do that in writing. Nobody can argue the gap between real and unreal anymore; see how fascinated we are with reality TV – there we watch the legends of others fail. To me it adds force to the end of an era. Today's myths and tricks, the structures of its fiction, are suddenly retro-kitsch. Security is retro-kitsch. The Hero is retro-kitsch.

But we have the choice. With an honest flexibility to chaos, with awareness, playfulness, a palate for insecurity, we could clear a new corner, leave the trap behind.

Distil fresh nuance and live in it.

The alternative is to board the departing myth and keep ramping up the Botox till we can't see through our cheeks. Or does society expect our fiction to support its fiction? Does it need it to?

I sense we'll soon find out.

Meanwhile I hope you made it through these motifs and

miniatures of accident, nature and legend.
    Okay, they don't follow what's expected.
    But when the fuck did we ever do that?

Because you're fucking worth it

The day before the skiing ban

Night

The sky rose glowing city-black, moth-eaten, till earlier coatings of night shone through in a blue of young flame. I was lit again after a long, deplorable state, heavy with all things of life, only grunting instead of speaking crisp words, not daring to care. My friend: the first thing is to arm a bacchanal. If we live half as angels and half as pigs, it's because we don't do the things that unite our halves. We live without commitment to ourselves, live adrift because the divine and the base within us are in conflict.

Life begs us to grasp it in a stranglehold.

The fingers of that grasp are our excesses.

So excess is a tool of life. Our use of it is key to advanced survival, which is survival in a dignified philosophical sense. And our ability to err towards it is nature's proof that it's our destiny.

Sparks fuming from under our suits, let's go forth.

Let's toast together and erode the thing.

Before it fucking corrodes.

Amen.

Quarantine

A short dialogue to reacclimatise with the derationalised zone:

PERSON A: 'Art surely favours states of mind where the intellect is disconnected, or at least dulled – wouldn't you say?'

PERSON B: 'Are you going to finish this beetroot or will I throw it out?'

PERSON A: 'Hm? Well I got it for that salad, but we need feta.'

PERSON B: 'And I suppose it's for me to get the feta.'

PERSON A: 'I didn't say that. I just said we needed it.'

PERSON B: 'Yes and it's just going to magically appear.'

PERSON A: 'I'll get some feta then.'

PERSON B: 'Oh for God's sake. I'll get it.'

PERSON C: 'Jesus wept.'

Younews

Ewwwwwww ashley gross!!!!!!!!!!!!!
Ewww lmfao : o

Petit Mal is a collection of short fictions, philosophical vignettes, and aphoristic interludes from the Man Booker Prize-winning author of *Vernon God Little*.

If you are familiar with the explosive End Times Trilogy (*Vernon God Little*, *Ludmila's Broken English*, *Lights Out in Wonderland*) by DBC Pierre, you will be well acclimatised to the heady heights traversed in this collection. Drawing on memoir and a life lived in pursuit of sensation, but always ignited by the flame of fiction, *Petit Mal* takes us further into the imagination of one of the most radically original prose stylists of the past decade.

Accompanied by dozens of illustrations and photographic 'evidence', the stories here inhabit worlds defined by appetite, excess and transcendence. Whether through food, drink, sex, drugs or a fantastic cocktail of all four, the impulse in this book is towards epiphany. And the inevitable hangover that follows. But even that (or those), in the world of DBC Pierre, can be nourishing.

'Pierre shreds the pretentious sophistication and fake joyousness of our Michelin-starred palaces, driving them to the ultimate conclusions of hedonism with a ferocity worthy of de Sade.'
Alan Warner, *Guardian*

DBC PIERRE won the Man Booker Prize and Whitbread First Novel Award for his debut, *Vernon God Little*. He lives in County Leitrim, Ireland.